SAY PLEASE

SAY PLEASE
LESBIAN BDSM EROTICA

EDITED BY
SINCLAIR SEXSMITH

CLEiS
PRESS

Published in the United States by Cleis Press, Inc., 2246 Sixth Street, Berkeley, California 94710.

Printed in the United States.
Cover design: Scott Idleman/Blink
Cover photograph: Hisayoshi Osawa/Getty Images
Text design: Frank Wiedemann
First Edition.
10 9 8 7 6 5 4 3 2 1

Trade paper ISBN: 978-1-57344-785-0
E-book ISBN: 978-1-57344-798-0

For my girl

Contents

INTRODUCTION

W hat is BDSM?

I thought this would be an easy question to answer. After all, I've been active in the kinky and queer worlds for many years, I've been reading erotica since I first got my hands on *My Secret Garden* by Nancy Friday when I was twelve years old, I've been writing erotica for longer than I've been sexually active, and I obsessed over lesbian erotica while I was coming out as queer in the late 1990s. But when I began sorting through the stories, reading nearly a hundred submissions, I started questioning what constituted BDSM in this specific context of lesbian erotica.

It is an acronym, multilayered, as some of its letters have multiple meanings: the BD is for bondage and discipline, the SM is for sadism and masochism, and the DS in the middle is also for domination and submission.

But it is more than that. As my definition widened, I started to see it as including all kinds of kink in general, the dozens of fetishes that get us hot and get our engines revving, our blood pumping. Certainly it includes good ol'-fashioned leather and whips and chains, the classic dungeon scenes like "A Public Spectacle" by D.L. King. And certainly it includes water sports, as in "The Keys" by Anna Watson, or vomiting from intense cocksucking, as detailed in "Purge" by Maria See. And I believe it also includes queering some classic domination and submission dynamics, like the femme daddy as in Alysia Angel's "Feathers Have Weight," and genderqueer boi submissives earning their right to flag black in Sassafras Lowrey's "Black Hanky." But how about a motorcycle, and a flogging and fucking on the back of a bike, as in Wendi Kali's "First Ride"? What about being bound and beaten with a hat, in Miriam Zoila Pérez's story "Baseball Cap"?

Certainly domestic discipline, domination, and submission, which are some of my personal favorite fantasies, in stories like "Gentleman Caller" by Sossity Chiricuzio, "Spoiled" by Shawna Elizabeth, "Housewife" by Gigi Frost, and "Counting Love" by August InFlux. I am always a sucker for beautifully described gender play, gender still being one of the things that gets me the most hot, and the conscious use of gender to heal and heighten intensity gets me going like nothing else can. The gender play and mindfulness in "Strong" by Xan West is exactly the kind of piece I mean.

Threesomes can certainly be broadly kinky, but are especially full of BDSM when they involve some sort of power play, or a technology service submissive as in "Going the Distance" by Elaine Miller, or a public humiliation scene at a bar like "Taking Direction" by Vie La Guerre. Sensation play seems key to me in BDSM: the stimulation from subtle to bold, from pinpricks to knives to floggers or even skilled bare-assed spankings, as in Dusty Horn's "Spanking Booth." Sensation can be used as a healing tool, too, as in BB Rydell's story "Call Me

Sir," which takes a different approach to the aftermath of police violence. Face slapping can be a hard limit or the most delicious sensation one craves, as Rachel Kramer Bussel's protagonist in "A Slap in the Face." Restraints, too, are imperative in BDSM, be they mental or psychological bondage such as in "The Cruelest Kind" by Kiki DeLovely or actual restraints on bondage furniture like a Saint Andrew's Cross in "Coming of Age" by Dilo Keith, a leather bench in "All of Me" by Amelia Thornton, or a sawhorse in "Three Weeks and Two Days" by Meridith Guy. Or it could be a combination of sensation, domination, discipline, and bondage, as described in "Unworthy As I Am" by Elizabeth Thorne.

I'm thrilled to have immersed myself in the kinky BDSM lesbian erotica submissions that came through my in-box and to have emerged with twenty-three stories with a huge range of sensation, discipline, bondage, topping, bottoming, submission, power, sadism, masochism, surrender, and fetish. This collection includes writers whose names you will probably recognize, writers who are new to publishing erotica, and quite a few who have never been published before.

As with many things, the more I look closely at BDSM, the harder it is for me to bring my flogger down on it and define precisely what I think it means. But I do think this anthology begins to explore the depth and breadth of experiences that this kinky queer world has to offer.

Sinclair Sexsmith
New York City

BASEBALL CAP

Miriam Zoila Pérez

From the moment we walked into the hotel room and I caught a glimpse of that wide cherry red wooden headboard, I knew exactly where I wanted her later. Our pre-dinner shower, our stroll around historic Savannah, our leisurely dinner and dessert were all colored by my building desire, my thoughts about what I would do with her when we got back to the room.

The excitement quietly builds, and I choose not to share my plans, knowing the surprise and giving of orders will turn her on. We get back to the room, giddy and full with each other. We play around on the bed, making out, teasing. I take her shirt off, and the sight of her full breasts pouring out of the top of her black lace bra sends a spark down to my crotch. I let her climb on top of me and release the bra clasp with one hand. She straddles my torso, upright on her knees, and I look up at the headboard behind me, picturing her splayed out against it. I cup her soft breasts in my hands, gently teasing her nipples to erection with my thumb and forefinger.

I ask her if she can grab onto the headboard. She grins at me, slight confusion in her eyes building to excitement as she realizes where my plans might take us. She easily grabs the top of it, arms wide, hands gripping the flat side of the wood framing the headboard. Perfect. *Stay where you are,* I tell her as I slide out from under, catching the scent of her sweetness as I pass between her legs. *Keep your back turned and take off your pants,* I tell her. She likes it when I give directions—obeying without a word, stripping down to just her boy-cut white underwear. They ride her wide sexy hips perfectly.

The sight of her half-naked body, her smooth ass and gentle hips, excites me more. I pause for a moment, taking her in, savor her waiting and wanting. She's a good girl—already positioned back with her hands on either side of the wide headboard, just her bra and underwear, eyes tightly shut. I gather my props, finding my weathered Nationals baseball cap on the floor by the bed next to my brown silk tie.

I climb up on the bed, easing up behind her and onto my knees. Even with her eyes closed she feels me coming closer, and her breath quickens in response. She sighs excitedly as I drag the silk tie across her breasts. I wrap it around her torso, running it along her body gently at first and then rougher, teasing her nipples back to attention with it.

I fold the tie up and gently hit her with it. I've never hit her before, so it feels charged with the electricity of newness. I drag it along her back and ass. I swing the tie faster, making a gentle whipping sound as it hits her backside. She moans, sucks in her breath.

I move the tie up, wrapping it around her wrists and bringing her hands together in the middle of the headboard, still gripping the top with her fingers. I know she likes to be restrained, and seeing her there—captive—makes my clit throb. I pick up my hat and start gently hitting her with it, first one side of her ass and then the other. Picking up confidence and speed, I hit her harder. She moans with pleasure, eyes closed, ass swaying. I straddle her from behind, pulling her ass down onto me. I rub my hands along her body, thrust up against her, hinting at what both she and I know is coming. We move together. I spread open her ass cheeks, grinding and pounding against her.

I grab her by the hair and pull her head back toward me, biting her neck. I whisper in her ear—*stay right here*—and wrench myself away from her. Climbing off the bed, I find my black leather case lying next to it in our jumble of clothes, grabbing my cock and harness. I take off my pants and underwear but leave on the button-down shirt I picked out to wear for dinner. I take my sweet time slipping the cock on, knowing that her excitement and anticipation are swelling, growing.

Finally I roll the condom on, climb back onto the bed where she is still waiting, hands restrained above her head, leaning against the headboard, ass in the air. I pull down her underwear and toss them off the bed. I can see her wetness; she's dripping from our play, from the anticipation of my cock inside her.

I straddle her ass, spreading my knees, and tease her wet lips with the tip of my cock. She moans quietly, arching her ass up toward me, and I enter her, swiftly, and a load moan escapes her lips. I thrust deep inside her, moving my body against hers, forcing her chest flat up against the headboard, my weight sandwiching her.

My cock is deep inside and I can feel her slick, wet pussy trembling. I grab onto the headboard on either side of her restrained wrists, bracing myself, pounding into her even harder. I grunt, feeling my orgasm building, overtaking me as I cry out, coming into her, out of breath.

FIRST RIDE

Wendi Kali

I don't remember the last time I took someone for a ride on my motorcycle. As I finished up the oil change on the last car of the day, I recalled the way her eyes lit up when I told her about my bike while I walked her home after our date last week. We had been dating for a few months, but since it was the end of winter, I hadn't mentioned the bike until that night. Winters in Oregon don't exactly allow for casual rides due to the unpredictable weather, so my bike had been weatherized and was sitting quietly in my garage.

Sara had only been with one other woman before me, so we talked a lot about the things she wanted to experiment with sexually. I was, of course, open to anything. During one of those late-night conversations, the subject turned to BDSM. She confessed that she had always wanted to be chained up, flogged, then fucked with a strap-on.

"You've never been fucked with a strap-on?" I asked.

"No. My first girlfriend wasn't much into toys," she

explained. "I asked her several times if she would just use them on me, but she had absolutely no interest in it."

"Being chained up and flogged requires a lot of trust from the person in the chains. I would be happy to indulge your fantasies when you feel that level of trust with me," I replied in my most gentlemanly manner.

She felt comfortable and trusted me enough to talk about it, which led me to believe that she trusted me enough to let me help make her fantasy come true.

After telling her about the bike during our last date, she confessed another fantasy:

"I've always wanted to ride on one, but never trusted anyone enough to actually do it."

"Oh really?"

"Yeah. I mean, you're putting your life in someone else's hands when you get on one of those."

"You have a point. You're not the one in control if you're on the back of the bike."

"Exactly. But, on the other hand, the danger of it gets me, well, excited," she said, looking up at me shyly.

She held my gaze for a moment to make sure I understood her.

"I see. You know, I would be happy to take you out on a slow and gentle ride through the country this weekend," I replied.

"Hmmm. I don't really have the patience for slow and gentle. I'm more of a fast-and-rough kind of woman, if you know what I mean," she said.

Looking at this beautiful woman standing before me in a low-cut dress, knee-high black leather boots, and black leather wrist cuffs, it took me a moment to think about what she had just said. Suddenly it clicked. Gazing at her bright red lips as they turned upward into a shy smile, I realized that she was looking for more than one kind of ride.

"I know exactly what you mean. I'll pick you up at two on Saturday," I said.

She smiled that beautiful smile that had already turned this hard, old butch to mush, then kissed me hard and hungrily before saying good night.

When I finally arrived at her place to pick her up, she greeted me at the door. "Are you ready for your first ride?" I asked.

Giggling nervously, she replied with a barely audible "Yes."

After leading her out to the bike, I stood behind her for a moment as she prepared to mount the powerful machine. The combination of her black leather boots, tight-fitting jeans, and the black mesh riding jacket I had just handed her made my blood race to all the right places.

Before she slid her helmet over her long, dark curls, I walked up behind her, slipped my arm around her waist, and whispered in her ear, "It's okay, baby. Just hold on tight and Daddy will take good care of you."

I could feel her body tremble as she leaned back against me and whispered, "Yes, Daddy."

After lowering her foot pegs, I climbed on and pressed the ignition button. The bike fired up with a roar. I extended my hand to her. She grabbed it for balance and climbed on behind me, wrapping those beautiful legs around me and the machine. She snuggled up as closely as she could against my back, slid her arms around me, and held on tightly.

I started off slowly through the quiet neighborhood streets so she could get a feel for the bike and how it rode. After a few minutes I could feel her begin to relax a bit, so I headed for the winding country road that would lead us to a secluded spot I had eyed many times while out riding.

The weather was perfect; the sun was shining and the breeze was gentle. When we reached the open road, I pulled back on the throttle and let the bike speed up a bit. Her grip around my waist went tight, then began to relax again. I patted her hands with one of mine, letting her know she was okay.

With each curve of the road, she became more and more comfortable with the ride and slowly let her hands travel down to my legs. I felt her pause for a moment when she felt my cock under the denim. She squirmed a little in her seat before squeezing and stroking it.

I could feel her want as she gripped and stroked the inside of my thighs. She may have been scared, but it was clear that fear combined with the feel of my cock was making her hot and needy. I grabbed her hands and returned them to my stomach, then patted them as if to say, *Patience, baby. Patience.*

We were close to the spot I'd chosen, which was good because I was ready to give her what she so badly wanted.

Coming out of the last curve, I turned off the road and into the field, parking under an old tree. We were secluded from the road in the middle of nowhere.

After climbing off the bike, I told her to take her jacket off, and being the good girl she is, she obeyed. While watching her, I slowly removed mine and hung them both on the handlebars.

She began to walk toward me, but I stopped her by holding up my hand.

"Take off your shirt," I ordered in a deep, commanding voice. Daddy had taken over.

She thought about protesting for a moment, but the demanding look I gave her led her to do as she was told.

"Now turn around and put your hands on the seat of the bike."

The sight of her long, dark curls flowing down her creamy back and gently touching the waist of her jeans made my pants feel a bit tighter as my clit grew harder and pushed against my cock. I walked up behind her and pushed her soft, dark hair to the side, unclasped her bra, and slowly pushed it down her arms while I leaned into her. When she felt my cock push against her ass, she pushed back against it hungrily.

Reaching into my saddlebags, I pulled out the wrist cuffs and chains. The rattle of the chains made her gasp with anticipation. I thought back to what she'd said on our last date about not having much patience for slow and gentle and used this little piece of information to tease and taunt her while reaching around her to slowly put her wrists in the cuffs.

Attaching the chains to the cuffs, I locked one of her beautiful wrists to the back of the bike and the other to the front. With her arms stretched out to her sides and her hair flowing gently in the breeze, she was a vision of beauty. Her back was my canvas.

I slid my hands around the curve of her hips and up to her belly—her skin was incredibly soft. My want for her grew as I grabbed her hips and pulled her hard against my cock.

She pushed against me and moaned a barely audible "Please, Daddy? Please fuck me."

"No," I growled in her ear while unbuttoning her pants and sliding my hands inside to her soft mound.

I could feel her warmth and wetness begging me to explore as she squirmed.

"Don't move," I ordered. She stopped with a whimper. The look of agony on her face was my prize.

"Plea—"

"Shhh. No."

Gliding my finger across her clit, I found her sweet center and slowly separated her lips to find her drenched. Dipping one finger into her warm wetness, I felt her knees buckle slightly. My grip around her waist grew tighter. She moaned even louder as I slid my finger back across her clit, covering it in her juices.

Still holding on to her and pressing my cock against her ass, I brought my finger up to my mouth to savor her sweetness. A low, almost evil chuckle escaped my lips as I reached into the saddlebag again. It was time for her beating.

"Your safeword is *ride*," I whispered in her ear before stepping back.

The black leather flogger was heavy in my hand as I whipped it around in the air for a moment to let her know what was coming. My eyes traveled to the small of her back. The surge of power I felt as I whipped the flogger around in the air was intoxicating. She put all of her trust in me for that moment.

Damn, she is beautiful.

I imagined the marks I was about to leave on her back as I readied her with soft, methodic taps with the strands of the flogger.

Gentle *tap, tap, taps* turned into hard *thud, thud, thuds*. Then with a loud smack the first marks appeared on her back. A slight scream escaped her lips while her arm muscles flexed as she pulled on the chains. Then more gentle *tap, tap, taps*, and hard *thud, thud, thuds* just before the loud crack of the strands against her back. Again leaving marks.

I could see her knees begin to get weak as the beating continued. Little beads of sweat rolled down her back and arms as she pulled on the chains and squirmed against the bike. Admiring my artistic work in the red markings that were growing on her back, I repeated the rhythm a few more times until more red welts appeared and I was satisfied with my masterpiece.

Returning the flogger to my saddlebag, I slowly moved my hands down her back to ease the stings my work brought. She was breathing hard and pushing against my hands. A slight moan escaped her lips.

"Please, Daddy," she pleaded.

"Please what, baby? Tell me what you want," I whispered in her ear.

"Please fuck me," she begged.

I slowly unbuttoned my 501s so she could hear them coming undone. She squirmed against me at the sound of one button after another.

Pulling my cock out and tightening up my harness, I let the tip of the cock tease her ass through her jeans. Her begging and squirming continued, and so did my teasing.

I unchained her from the bike and turned her around to face me. She looked up at me with her pleading eyes.

"Take off your boots and your pants," I ordered.

She obeyed and stood before me completely naked with her long hair blowing gently in the breeze. Her nipples were hard and reaching for me. The creamy curves of her body begged for my touch.

"Come here, baby."

Cupping her face in my hands, I looked into her pleading eyes and couldn't help but kiss her. I was gentle at first, then hungrily bit her lips while she begged with her moans.

Finally, I wrapped my arms around her and pulled her up onto my cock. She wrapped her legs and arms around me and held on tightly as my cock slid easily into her warm wetness. Hungrily taking in all of my cock, she tried to ride me. I grabbed her ass and pulled her to me to stop her.

Looking down at me she pleaded, "Please, Daddy. Please make me come."

I smiled wickedly, then carried her over to my bike. Still holding on to her, I threw my leg over the bike and straddled it. Her ass sat on the fuel tank as she leaned back against the handlebars. I started to fuck her with a slow rhythm that gradually became faster and harder.

"Oh fuck, Daddy! Yes! Fuck me!" she screamed.

"Yes, baby. Ride my cock. Come for me, baby. Come for Daddy."

I thrust my cock into her wetness as hard and as deeply as I could until the screams of climax escaped her lips, screams so loud they echoed through the trees.

She fell back into my arms, and I held her there while the aftershocks of her climax shuddered through her beautiful body. I gently kissed her neck, then nibbled on her ear as she leaned against me and wrapped her arms around my neck.

"How was your first ride, baby?" I whispered in her ear.

"Mmm...even better than I'd imagined. Thank you, Daddy. Can we do it again?" she asked with a smile.

"Yes, baby. Daddy would love to take you on another ride."

A SLAP
IN THE FACE

Rachel Kramer Bussel

Jade strolled into the bar, walked straight up to Amber, who was leaning against it wearing a slinky leopard-print slip, ripped fishnet stockings, a see-through black top along with a sheer black bra, and dangerously tall black heels, her red hair gleaming even in the low lights, and slapped her across the face. The sound was louder than Jade had expected, the sting in her palm stronger, both of which she liked. Amber didn't smile, not with her mouth, anyway, but Jade knew exactly how much she'd liked the slap. She could read it in the way Amber shivered, the way Amber's eyes skittered from the ground and, for a second, up to hers, from the way her body radiated a heady combination of fear, awe, and desire.

This was not a kinky bar. It wasn't a dyke or queer bar, either. It was your average Brooklyn dive bar, filled with its mix of colorful high-glam hipsters in everything from hot pants to schoolgirl skirts, older white guys with huge beer steins who seemed like they'd been sitting there since before either woman was born, parents stealing a late-night cocktail before the baby-sitter had to go home. And Jade and Amber had shared a stormy, kinky relationship of six months, one that Jade wanted to last even though she had no idea if they would blaze through all the intense passion zinging between them too fast and have nothing left, or if they could find ways to keep it going. She was trying to live in the moment, and this scene was part of her new mission. She kept any trembling she felt on the inside steady as she stared down at the girl who'd given so much of herself, but was always looking to give more.

To anyone watching, it would've looked like what it was: a slap in the face, a blow across her cheek, something at least a little mean, harsh, powerful, something that must have hurt and brought tears to Amber's eyes. And it was, certainly, all of those things—Jade would never have denied that it was one of the most powerful ways you could strike someone—but it wasn't unwanted; in fact, Amber thought it was the hottest thing she'd ever done, and she'd been to, and participated in, her share of extreme play parties. She looked up at Jade and realized that her fantasies had been fulfilled, technically, but not all the way; her face tingled in anticipation of the next slap. She suddenly wished she'd worn her matching leopard-print panties, the silky ones that rode up her ass, because her wetness was starting to trickle down her thigh. She liked it, even more than when Jade slapped her at home; she liked it so much she was torn between step-ping between Jade's jeans-clad legs and pressing their bodies tight together and what she wound up choosing, looking right up into her girlfriend's eyes, letting her see the tears that shim-mered there.

"You want me to slap you again, don't you?" Jade's voice was low, deep, quiet enough that only Amber could hear. Jade kept the tremor out of it, the awe that this creature was letting her do the most wicked things to her and kept wanting to push the envelope.

"Yes, Jade, I do." Amber let a tear fall because she didn't totally understand why she liked it, she just knew she did, and she wanted people to know. Well, that wasn't strictly true. She couldn't honestly say she wanted people to know about her predilection for being smacked, but the fact that now, finally, they did, after so many months of fantasizing, made her pussy feel like it was both tightening and expanding all at once.

This time, Jade tenderly held her hand against one of Amber's cheeks, the pristine one, and with the other raked her short nails down the edge of the other. She waited, toying with her, trying to ignore their surroundings, because the exhibitionism was really Amber's thing, though she couldn't deny she got a small thrill from being so controlling in so public a location. Then she did it again, a smack that reverberated through her palm, skin striking skin, and again. Jade stepped forward and shoved her knee between Amber's legs, pressed her mouth against her ear. "Thank me for it, or I won't do it again."

"Thank you, Jade. I love you." Amber hadn't meant to say that, but it came out in a rush. There were moments when she was afraid of Jade, but she liked those moments, she liked the way those moments spurred her on to be more daring, to let herself get pushed farther off what felt like a precipice, until everything she had was Jade's for the taking.

"Let's go," Jade said, plucking Amber's half-full glass from her hand and placing it on the bar, then rushing her outside, while Amber scrambled to put her pink fake-fur coat back on before they entered the chilly night. Jade would've stayed, but what was bubbling up inside her was too fierce for public consumption. There's no way the patrons of that bar would ever have understood what she wanted to do to Amber; the truth was, she hardly understood it herself, but she knew it filled something primal within her, something that made her feel like she was enacting an ancient ritual, a hunt-or-be-hunted animalistic desire to go for the kill. Slapping Amber, beating her, tying her down, choking her, all took Jade's breath away as much as they did Amber's, though she didn't have the freedom to show it quite as much. "Why are you shaking?" Amber had once asked after a particularly cruel, intense scene. Jade had just shaken her head, not having any further answer.

This time, she wanted Amber quiet, even though she usually loved the noises the girl made. She pulled Amber into an alley she'd scoped out beforehand. The wind whipped around them as Jade pressed Amber against the brick, then slapped her face as hard as she could. Amber let out a cry, her nostrils flaring, her body straining against its own desires. Jade knew there was a part of Amber that was horrified at just how much she liked being slapped, and an even bigger part that was in awe of how little it took for the sensitive skin on her face to make her dizzyingly wet. Amber liked to be hit all over her body, but there were some spots she liked best. Her face. Her pussy. Her tits, especially the nipples, all areas Jade had mostly shied away from with her previous play partners, by request.

Amber wanted it, and the first time she'd done it, Amber had come with a ferociousness Jade had never seen, while her own arousal had been different than anything that had come before. "I want you to walk up to me at a bar and slap my face, so everyone can see," Amber had e-mailed her a month ago, and ever since, Jade had been fantasizing about doing just that. Now that she had, she wanted so much more. She wanted someone to help her, but that would have to happen another time. For now it was just the two of them, ready for anything.

"Put your hands above your head," Jade said, partly to see if

Amber would do it, partly to watch her breasts thrust forward with the movement. "Good girl," she told her. She looked closely at her girlfriend's beautiful face, so pale, so sensitive. The wind was competing with her hand in coloring her flesh, but Jade didn't mind. It had taken her a while to get used to the fact that she liked slapping Amber, liked hurting her, liked seeing the tears rush to her eyes as she looked up at her so desperately.

Amber was biting her lower lip, and Jade used her fingers to pry her lips apart. "You told me you want this, Amber. If you flinch or fidget or look like you don't, I'm not going to do it."

"I do want it," Amber exclaimed, the words tripping over themselves. "I want you to slap me. I want you to hurt me. I want you to slap me so hard my ears ring." Amber kept looking up at Jade even though Jade sensed she wanted to close her eyes, to pretend that somehow it wasn't her saying those perverse, filthy words. Because they were extremely perverse; asking to be slapped made it all completely real. Amber couldn't pretend Jade was some dominating brute, at least, not entirely.

Jade liked it when Amber watched, when Amber saw her hand coming, when she anticipated the pain. "I have a present for you," she said, and reached into her jeans pocket, the jangling of the clamps loud in her ears. Amber's eyes widened, and the hint of fear Jade saw, the hint that warmed her heart even as she prepared to tighten them around Amber's nipples, made Jade smile. Amber was so open, whether by choice or design or a little of both; she could never hide her feelings, not like some girls Jade had played with who only truly let go when they were under the most extreme erotic distress. Jade could play the too-cool-for-school game too—but she didn't want to.

She leaned down and pressed her body tight against Amber's, kissing her roughly. "Take out your tits," she said, "and hurry, or I'll have to do it for you." They both knew that "do it for you" was code for "rip your top off and send all the tiny buttons flying to the floor," because Jade had done it before, with a hundred-dollar top (though she'd bought a replacement for Amber later). Still, Amber rushed to unbutton her blouse and take out her breasts as soon as Jade stepped back to give her room, and the sight floored Jade, even though she'd seen those glorious globes so many times before. There was still something awe-inspiring about their weight, their eagerness to be touched and abused. Amber's tits were like a work of art, and were Jade's favorite part of her body. "Pinch those nipples for me," Jade said, allowing Amber to bring her hands down. Amber started to lightly grab them between her thumbs and forefingers, much too lightly for Jade.

"No," she said fiercely. "Pinch them. Like this." And with that she slapped Amber's hands away and pinched and pulled at the same time, then twisted, watching Amber's face contort as she did, knowing it was making her wet, knowing too that the longer she did it, the more Amber was contemplating using her safeword, "strawberry," a fruit she hated but ate when it was the only polite thing to do. Similarly, Amber hated to have to resort to her safeword, and only had once, when her leg cramped up.

When Jade was done, she let Amber's breasts go, watching them bounce lightly before settling where they should be. Then she clamped one hand over Amber's mouth and slapped her tits, slapped them hard enough to feel the sting in her right palm, to see the marks on Amber's breasts, a defiant red. This brought out the wild beast in Jade, the one who wanted to claw and bite and grind Amber into the ground, the one that liked watching her struggle, feeling her lips pressing against her hand as she then switched to flicking her middle finger against her thumb and then right at the bull's-eye of each nipple.

She finally let go, both of them breathing heavily. "Now

you're ready," Jade said, and Amber gave her another of those almost painful looks, one that seemed to beg her not to put the clamps on while also swearing she'd leave her if she didn't. Jade took Amber's now-sore nipples, one at a time, and attached the clamps, pushing the rubber-covered lever just a little bit higher than she knew Amber would have, before taking the metal chain holding them together and shoving it into Amber's mouth. "Bite down hard, sweetie, because if you let go, I'm out of here." She slapped her face again, to see what Amber would do. She bit down harder on the chain, breathed in deeply through her nose.

And then Jade went to work on Amber's pussy. She hadn't intended, originally, to go this far in public. They'd been outside long enough that they could, reasonably, be noticed, and Amber was a knockout even when they weren't doing anything out of the ordinary, drawing catcalls and sometimes a little too much attention. But Jade couldn't have stopped herself from reaching between her girlfriend's legs and slipping her fingers inside her if she'd wanted to. Of course Amber wasn't wearing panties, and of course Amber was wet. Jade looked up, looked at Amber's eyes—full, wide, riveted on hers, her teeth clamped around the metal chain, her body saying, in a language that needed no words, *Take Me.* And Jade did, no longer on quite the power trip she'd been on before, but now intent on giving something back.

She worked her fingers in the familiar ways she'd grown to learn Amber liked, navigating her insides, feeling her press back against her in response. Usually this was when Amber let out a stream of dirty words, or Jade did, or both of them did, but this time, Jade was silent as she pushed three fingers deep into Amber's pussy, and then four, because she needed to be as far as she could go. She felt a slight twinge in her wrist as she shifted, sinking to her knees so she could peek up Amber's skirt; the sight of her hand in Amber's cunt never failed to make her swell with pride. She kept going, not needing to rattle the chain, not needing to slap or hit or hurt Amber any more, because she knew Amber could still feel the glow of the pain, the sweet sting from getting exactly what she wanted. Then Jade couldn't resist, and pressed her head against Amber for a quick taste of her clit, a quick suck on her engorged bud that had Amber twisting her hips in response.

That was what did it; that stroke of her tongue had Amber coming hard, coming so she crushed Jade's hand just the way she liked it. When Jade felt Amber relax, she pulled her hand out, then got out a wet wipe, because she was a top who came prepared. "Let go," she said, taking the chain from Amber's teeth with her own, both of them still hungry. She released the clamps slowly, heard Amber's loud gasp as the blood rushed back into her nipples. Jade untied Amber's wrists and pulled her clothes back in place. They'd been out there maybe ten minutes, Jade guessed; not long, but enough time to do what she needed to do. Jade took Amber's hand and led it between her legs. She was packing. She kept it there as they walked home, where it would be Jade's turn to get exactly what she wanted.

HOUSEWIFE

Gigi Frost

for Mel

I flip through the hangers, passing over black knit skirts and clingy print dresses, looking for something in cotton that's not totally wrinkled, and find a pink dress with scalloped edges, short sleeved, a thrift-store find passed on from a friend, which I've never worn. I hang it in the bathroom and start the shower. Under too-hot water I run my hand over my cunt, feeling the swelling of my labia. I've been turned on all day, taking frequent breaks from data entry to masturbate on my bed, thinking about begging for forgiveness under her hand.

Stockings first, then garter belt, then panties. I slide slippers on over my seamed stockings and boil potatoes, slice tofu, rub a loaf of bread with garlic and olive oil. The timing of dinner is tricky. When it's half-finished I fix my hair, change into heels, and put on lipstick and powder. She texts me when she gets off the subway. I spend five more minutes on the computer, then shut it down and return to the kitchen. I let myself make a mess, bang pots and pans around, get out the gin and a cheap pink cocktail shaker my sister gave me for my birthday. I've never made a martini before, but she's a confirmed beer drinker and not an expert at drinking them, either.

I hear her at the door, making more noise than is needed with her keys. I pour the drink with shaking hands and open the door. Seeing her, it's hard to stay in character, hard not to throw my arms around her and ask about her day supervising the queer legal counseling line.

"Hi, honey." She takes the drink, cups my face with her other hand for a kiss. "How's my beautiful wife?"

"I, um. Why don't I take your bag and you can have your drink in the living room while I finish dinner?"

"It's not ready?" Her face is taking on a dark expression, clouding over the jovial-husband act. But underneath all that is a wisp of a smile. I have to be careful not to laugh. The whole thing is so scripted, so trite. But these tired lines are a key to our desire, another path to having each other in exactly the way we need.

I hold on to my nervous expression and look at my feet. "I burned the garlic the first time, and the potatoes took forever. It will be done in a minute. I'll bring you the paper, okay?" Again, her expression wavers. Not trusting herself to speak, she grunts and hands me her bag and coat, turning toward the living room. I hang her coat in the bedroom and leave her bag at the foot of the bed.

As we sit down at the table, the silence is electric between us. We've both been working all day and we need to eat, but we want to get on with this. I take a few bites, push food around my plate, make a show of nervous conversation, twirl my hair around my fingers.

She slides her plate away and stands suddenly. "Come with me. You can clean this up later."

"Can I make you another drink?"

"You heard what I said." Her deliberate, harsh tone fills me with dread and anticipation. I follow her. She sits on the couch, martini glass on the coffee table before her, and pats the seat next to her. "This isn't the first time."

"The first time what?"

"This isn't the first time you've been late with dinner. In fact, it's more like the fourth or fifth."

"I'm sorry, I'm trying—" I begin, but she interrupts, her hand on my shoulder.

"Listen to me. I work hard all day so I can take care of you. Aren't you happy? Don't I give you everything you want? I don't ask much from you. All I want is for dinner to be ready when I get home. Is that so hard?"

"No, but I—"

"Is it going to happen again?"

"No, I'll make sure it doesn't."

"I don't believe you. We've talked about this before, and look what just happened. But I have a way to make sure it doesn't happen again."

I put my hand on her shoulder. "Please, sweetheart, I'll be sure it doesn't happen again."

"No, I said *I'm* going to be sure it doesn't happen again."

"What do you mean?"

"Stand up." I look her in the eyes and obey, slowly. I am so wet, both because I know what's about to happen and because it's so hot to pretend I have no idea. "Lift your dress up."

"What are you doing?"

"I'm making sure you remember to have dinner ready on time. Come here." I edge closer and she bends me over her lap. She caresses my ass. "Do you know what I'm going to do?"

"You can't do this."

"I can and I will. You're my wife and I have every right to teach you a lesson." She pauses. "I'm going to hit you ten times." The thrill of wanting to be spanked and the dissonance of pretending I don't, the pull of my garters against my ass, the hardness of her cock. She's not hitting me as hard as she could, but I know she wants me to struggle. And this character I'm playing would struggle, so I moan and kick.

I imagine this woman, this young wife. I've been thinking about her all day. When my mind turns to consent, misogyny, how fucked up this fantasy is, I push those thoughts aside and remember how hot this makes me. We live in this society every day, breathing in misogyny and homophobia and gender policing with the very air. The least we can do is get off on it.

So I imagine myself nervous, in love, resentful of this new direction my husband is taking. Surprised at how this is turning me on. Excited and revolted by her cock as it hardens against my thigh.

She tells me to stand, moves me onto an armchair, my face toward the wall, on my knees. She arranges my dress above my waist, draped over the chair. "I'm going to leave you here to think about what you've learned tonight. Then I'm going to come back and see if you've learned your lesson. Don't move."

I give a slight nod and breathe in sharply. She pats my ass and I hear her in the kitchen, piling up plates and pans, wiping down the table.

When I hear her approach, I don't move, but I feel the charge between us, like air pressure dropping before a storm. She comes close and I flinch. She slides her hands up my thighs, between my labia.

"Why are you wet?"

"I...I don't know. I think I'm wet because you spanked me."

"I'm going to punish you for this. Get on your knees."

I stand, ungraceful in my heels, and kneel.

"Take off my belt."

I fumble again. All my poise vanished hours ago in a turned-on haze.

"Give me your hands." She wraps the belt around them, then takes out her cock and pulls my head in. "You're going to suck my cock now. You're going to show me how much you want me. You're going to show me how grateful you are that I taught you a lesson."

I love this. And, just a little, I hate it. Hate how unyielding her cock is, hate how I can't quite manage to swallow it. And just when I'm getting the hang of it, just when my mouth and gag reflex are surrendering to her, it's over. She's pulling out, untwisting her belt from my wrists, and throwing me on the floor. I grind my hips against the cold wood, my clit burning. I'm so turned on that I barely register the blows from her belt as pain. I feel burning, sharp caresses, from the top of my ass to my thighs. This is all I want. I could take this forever, but she stops and tells me to get on my hands and knees.

She fucks me like I don't matter, like I really am her property, her chattel, there for her pleasure and nothing else. And this fucking ultimately makes me come like nothing else can, it's better than anything more comfortable or tender or aligned with what I might ask for if given a chance.

She pulls out and I collapse on the floor. This is the moment when I can roll over, smile sweetly, and reach my arms up to her, my stern top, my fantasy husband, my handsome gentle girlfriend. But she's pushed me so far, I don't want to leave this submissive place just yet.

Last night, lying with my head on her shoulder, she told me about her childhood fantasies, rescuing princesses and then ravishing them.

"The princess really wants you to fuck her, but you sort of have to make her," she said.

I love being her princess.

She's kneeling behind me still, breathing hard, putting her cock back into her briefs.

"Thank you, sir. Please, sir, I need more. Please fuck my ass, sir."

She reaches around for my nipple and twists. "You dirty slut. You need me to fuck you in the ass? Go lie down on the bed."

She follows me into the room with lube and water, offers it to me; I smile and drink but keep my head bowed. I've gone so deep I don't even want the interval of equality and real life that sometimes comes with a break for water.

"If you want your ass fucked, you're going to have to take more. You still need to be punished for moving your hips earlier. Did you think I missed you grinding your dirty little clit into the floor? Slut."

"Yes sir, I'm sorry, sir. Please punish me, sir."

"Get over my lap."

"I'm going to spank you again, but first I'm going to put this in your ass. You need to remember that all your holes belong to me." We've left the housewife scenario behind us, I realize, as she lubes up the plug and opens me, leaving me squirming and begging for another spanking, for her to pinch my nipples again, for as much pain and humiliation as she wants to give me.

The spanking is almost too much on top of the strapping I received earlier, but I can tell she wants to give it to me, and her hot breath, her need to take me, carry me up and over and I come under her hand.

CALL ME SIR: A SMUTTY PULP FICTION TALE

BB Rydell

I stare at my fingertips while Jake Six chats me up. She's been riding my jock with her yap for nearly twenty minutes now. Crowing on about the string of former heartthrobs she's seduced in the past year. The firefighter who lived upstairs and undressed with the curtains open, the intrepid photographer with a bent for threesomes, the femme who made no apology for her incessant addiction to speed.

I motion to Martha for another bottle of Red Stripe and lean in closer to Jake. I'm looking at a carbon copy of myself ten years ago: the dyke who likes to use popularity as armor and bait simultaneously. I don't blame her. There is crazy drama in small queer communities. All of us are searching for ways to protect our soft hearts. Martha drops the beer by my hand. A sizz of sparkle escapes the pressurized cap when she opens it. I take a long drink and set it back down. Jake bends the black cocktail straw between her fingers; I watch a drop of whiskey bead onto her finger from the tip of the straw. I watch Jake lick the tip of her finger while she's watching me.

I rub my hand over the back of my shaved head. At least they left a little bit of hair on top, enough to grab. That's my rule.

The glittery red bar stool squeaks as I shift my weight and look toward the door: 11:46 p.m. My friends must be running late. It was their idea to meet here first before heading over to the Cuff. Where are they? I drop a napkin on the floor and lean over to pick it up so I can get a good look around the bar just in case they're lurking about. I don't need another pair of eyes on me tonight. Then again, my swipe at privacy is probably futile. You can't keep anything a secret in this bar.

"You're Jake, right?" I say, climbing back onto the stool. Jake shims the glass in her hands. Lazily eyes the amber liquid tracing over sweaty ice cubes.

I take another long swig of beer. "Nine-to-one odds you get what you want, don't you?"

"Oh yeah?" she rumbles. "Would you like to find out for yourself?" She unbuttons the top two buttons of her tight pea-green polo T-shirt and pushes up the sleeves.

"Nice ink," I say.

She's smirking again, cracking her knuckles one by one. I watch her hands and try to hold back a smile.

"Should I be afraid?" I say ruefully, carefully shedding the clammy label with my blunt fingernail.

She shifts her eyes to her shoulder. "I've got my uncle's brass knuckles permanently tattooed on my arm." Her voice rises, a coy smile covering her demeanor. She leans toward me and flirts. "Don't mess with me unless..."

I cut her off mid-sentence, push the bottle away, and thrust my hand out to grab her shirt. "Unless what? You wanna fight me, freshman?" I pull her closer. She swallows nervously, raises her eyebrows, tilts her head down, and smiles without showing teeth. "Go ahead," I growl cunningly. "All of your posturing, flexing, fucking around—that's not what you want. I don't care how many cocky smiles you've got hidden behind that grin."

She swallows again. I loosen my grip. A breath escapes her throat. Releasing my grip completely, I settle back into my stool. I choke the neck of my nearly drained beer, tilt it back to my throat, and watch her watching me swallow.

"I know what you want." I reach over to straighten out her shirt. "Thing is, you're going to have to be a good *boy* and learn some respect before anyone is going to give it to you." Jake swallows again while staring at my mouth. My friends walk through the door. I see them mingling in the corner.

I run my tongue over my lower lip and smile. She drops her gaze. "My friends are here. I have to get going. Tomorrow night, I'll be by around seven o'clock to give it to you. This is a one-time offer."

Rolling her eyes to focus on my mouth, she cocks her chin again and, with an I'm-gonna-knock-you-out expression of defiance, says, "Why the fuck not?"

The following night I show up at Jake's apartment, ready to teach her a lesson from my "finishing school." After a few knocks the door swings open. Jake is wearing a bright orange T-shirt snaking into retro faded gray low-rider jeans.

"I just got home from 'volunteering' downtown," she says with air quotes.

I read about the queer bashing in the Seattle *Stranger* last year. She punched out the attacker so her friends she was with could get away. That's what earned her all of those orange-shirted community service hours. The queer hater was set free.

She leads me to the living room. It's lit with candles. Pine-scented incense masks an underlying musty basement smell tickling my nostrils.

"I'll just go and change first." I block her path with my body.

Jake pushes my shoulders, "C'mon, let me by."

I hold her back.

"Orange becomes you," I say. She feigns boredom as I lean into her chest and scan the room for space. "Why don't you grab my toy bag over there and put it in the living room?" Rolling her eyes, she makes a W with her hands and mouths, "Whatever."

Struts over to the door, slings the bag over her right shoulder and lugs it over. I notice her bicep flexing under the weight.

"What do you have in here, anyway?" she asks.

I don't answer.

"Place the bag to my right and stand three feet in front of the sofa, facing the window."

She tugs on her belt, pulls up her jeans, and files into place.

"On your knees," I command.

Jake slowly drops to the floor. Raising her hand to cover her mouth. "Like this?" she mutters, stifling a laugh. Ignoring her brattiness, I pull my blue riding crop out of the bag and casually rap the stinging end of the whip in my hands.

I pace in front of her.

She stares at my faded, ripped blue jeans and scratched motorcycle boots.

"First: ground rules. You are to respect what I say. You will learn to anticipate me, but for now I will give you directions and you will follow them."

Jake murmurs something under her breath. I step closer to her and pull up a chair. My crotch is at the same level as her face. I lean in closer.

"Second rule: Don't think for one moment you're going to get away with any bullshit with me."

Jake raises her right hand to her forehead and salutes. "No bullshit. Got it."

"Third rule: Don't speak unless spoken to. The most important rule: Call me Sir."

A muffled growl hisses from Jake's mouth. Two fingers pressing underneath her chin, I coax her to standing and command her to get against the wall with her arms at her sides.

Casually, I say, "Tell me all the places you've fucked inside your apartment." She feels yoked by my request before another roll of cockiness covers her demeanor.

"I've fucked on my bed, in my bed, with my eyes open and closed…"

I stop her. "This lesson is called call me Sir. You will repeat your boastful sexcapades in military fashion and with proper intonation. Begin and end each of your sentences with 'Sir.'"

Jake shifts her weight from one foot to the other, drops her hip, and looks up at the ceiling. "What the hell? Are you going to chastise me all night?"

I walk directly in front of her, pull her head down so we are standing face-to-face. I skillfully trace her neckline with the flat end of the whip. A bead of sweat lingers on her brow. I pull out my trusty forest-green-colored hanky from my back pocket and wipe it off. She winces when I crack the whip on the wall right above her eye.

"If I want to chastise you all night, that's what I will do." I move closer, as if I were a field officer sharing a survival secret with a new recruit, and whisper, "You fuck with me again, we're done."

Jake's body reacts in a shudder. Stuffing the hanky back in my pocket, I turn and walk over to the window to compose myself.

I pull back the blinds.

A stealth femme is walking a three-legged Chihuahua on the sidewalk.

A red neon Coca-Cola sign flashes over an old-fashioned doorway.

The little fucker's obedient breathing pulls me back into the room.

With a shit-eating grin, I turn and walk toward her.

Jake punches the air like a cheerleader, rolls her eyes, and with a testy smile, spits: "Sir, I've fucked women on my bed, in my bed, with my eyes open and closed. I've fucked in my kitchen, bent them over my computer desk a few times. Sir. I even fucked a girl on my fixie over there in the corner."

Her gaze lingers straight at me while she flings a pointed finger to the corner where a shiny blue one-speed "fixie" bicycle leans against the wall.

"Are you a good fuck, loudmouth? Are you as good a fucker as you are a disrespectful bullshitter?"

"Better," she says defiantly.

What am I going to do with her!

"Okay," I say, "you obviously crave being broken. Show me where you sleep at night."

She leads me to her bedroom. We sit on her bed. I command her to wear a blindfold and strip down to her briefs. She strips clumsily, arms and legs flapping around, wrestling the orange T-shirt off and over her head. I notice a gallery of tattoos painted across her body. The one sprawling from the base of her armpit up a few inches and down the right side of her rib cage is my favorite. It's a giant octopus with crisscrossed pirate swords behind its placid head. One of the tentacles waves a tattered Jolly Roger skull-and-crossbones flag.

I hold out my hand and lead her from the bedroom over to the "fuck desk" she so confidently described a moment ago. I'm strapped under my jeans. I trace my finger along one of Mr. Octopus's stripy, black-patterned tentacles from her navel to her shoulder and push her to her knees in front of the desk chair, grabbing her modern mullet haircut with my fist.

"Tell me why you want me to do this. Be respectful." I squat down next to her ear and whisper, "I only fuck with respectful faggots. Are you a respectful faggot?"

"What the fuck do you mean, am I a respectable faggot?" she fangs.

"Correction. What the fuck do you mean, SIR." A fistful of hipster-than-thou hair twists in my fingers. I pull off her blind-fold, pushing her face down to my boots.

"Lick them," I command.

Smiling, she doesn't move a muscle. I can see fear steeped in attitude boiled hot to perfection in her eyes.

I repeat firmly, "Lick my fucking boots, loudmouth brat."

She bends forward, presses her dirty pink lips to my scratched-up boots. Even slips her bratty tongue around the toe of my left one.

"That's better." I pull her back to kneeling in front of me and stroke her hair. She breathes in through her nose and out her mouth. I'm standing directly in front of her, and I notice her eyes staring at my cock.

"You still want this?" I grab my crotch. "Yeah?" I move in front of her. I take a step back, ring my thumbs through the loops of my jeans, and flare out my fingers. "Now, let's see. Tell me why you want this."

Jake smiles, looks me up and down, and says, "Why do you care?" She winks.

Some loudmouths just don't ever learn, do they?

"Get against the wall."

She rises, hands to her sides.

"Are you forgetting something?" I ask.

Jake shifts her weight, puts her hands on the waistband of her underwear, and stares at the sofa in the corner.

"No. I'm following your orders."

"Eyes forward. You are following my orders, Sir! Say it."

She drops her hands and looks at me. "I am following your orders, Sir."

"Better," I sigh.

I walk over and push her up against the wall. She's facing me. I dip down into my bag and pull out a set of ankle spreaders: a two-foot metal bar with ankle restraints on either side. I take some rope and tie her wrists behind her back.

"Turn around and face the wall."

"Okay, fine, Sir," she spits as she turns to face the wall. I grab the spreaders and fasten them to her ankles. I take a piece of paper and move over to the wall.

"Hold this to the wall with your nose."

She wriggles her bound arms and shimmies her ankles before lowering into submission, uttering, "Yes, Sir."

I step back to look at my handiwork before reaching back into my toy bag and pulling out a copy of *Becoming a Police Officer: An Insider's Guide.*

"Remember to pay close attention to this lesson, little fucker. Now, I know that hot temper of yours has gotten you in trouble with the law. I've seen you downtown in your orange T-shirt ticking out community service hours. Sometimes the best cops are the ones who've been on both sides, if you know what I mean."

Jake grimaces. I notice the paper slip a bit.

I walk over, open the book, and read into her ear, "'Do you like the smell of danger, the victory of helping the helpless?'" She's turned on. Her heavy breathing and clenched jaw are dead giveaways.

"I like watching you squirm, little fucker."

Her nipples are getting harder by the second. She lets out a moan, starts shaking just a little bit. "Is my star pupil getting restless? Do you need to be steadied?"

I lean in and put my hot mouth just on the outside of her neck without actually contacting it. She's finding it difficult to control herself. Just as her ass starts to melt into my crotch behind her, I sink my teeth into her skin, slap her ass hard with the palm of my hand, and step back. She turns her head a little bit, trying to get a glimpse of me. The paper slips and nearly drifts to the floor.

"Tsk, tsk." I release her binds with one tug of the quick-release knot, unfasten the ankle spreader with my foot, and pull down her tight pink boi briefs. Sighing defeat, she steps out of her underwear and rests her forehead against the wall.

"Drop and give me twenty," I command.

Jake slaps the wall, turns, and drops to the floor.

I stand over her while her body dips up and down. I watch her arm muscles pulse. She's groaning like a boy now. Defiantly counting off: "Fifteen, sixteen, seventeen, eighteen..."

"Are you showing off for me now?"

"No, it's just that twenty push-ups are no problem for me. I want to do more."

"Get up," I demand.

She rises.

I move right in front of her face and shout, "You want to do more, what?"

"Sir!"

"This is the last fucking time I'm gonna say that. Get back against the wall."

I bind her wrists behind her back. Put the paper back under her nose. Casually dangle a set of nipple clamps connected by a heavy silver chain from my fingertips in her peripheral vision. Her left eye shifts suddenly to meet mine.

"You wanted more? Here you go."

I play with her nipples before securing the clamps one at a time on her red buds.

"Yes, Sir," she submits under her breath. I smile and continue.

"You like the police talk, don't you?"

Her shoulder twitches, her face falls. I can tell this is a mixed bag of emotions.

"You are a star faggot, aren't you? What we've got here is one law-abiding faggot."

"Sir, I am a fucking faggot."

A weary expression crosses her face. Her mood shifts. The paper flutters to the floor. I move over to her. Has she had enough? But then I notice her body flush with excitement. A dual effort like she's got a freight train running through her mind and a vibrator on her clit. Excitement trilled by vibes of fear. There were three people against the queer bashers that night, but she was the only one who got dragged down to the station. The cops saw her do it, and they profiled her because of the way she looked.

"Did the cops take you down that night?"

A tear escapes her eye.

She stammers. "Yes, Sir."

I feel suddenly awkward. It feels like I'm standing in the way of control. I can't go back in time and fix what happened in the past.

I slide the nipple clamps off. I notice the blood has drained from her hands and I loosen the rope that is binding her wrists to bring back circulation. I walk behind her and press my chest into her back. Wrap my arms around her and hold her in my arms like a long-lost friend found again.

Squeezing Jake's body gently, I say, "Tell me what happened that night."

Rubbing her wrists, she says, "Me and a bunch of my friends were on our way home. Some men started yelling at us. They were calling us dykes, spitting at us. Then two cops came, a woman and a man. They let the others go but they grabbed me." She rubs her brass knuckle tattoo and chuckles. "I guess I looked like trouble."

"Cops can be ugly," I say. "Serve and protect—so long as you look the part."

She twitches a bit, but there is a new light in her eye.

"They yelled really loud, and when I yelled back the man cop told the woman to 'get ready,' and the next thing I knew I had the wind knocked out of me and my face was on the sidewalk and my arms and legs were tied together with a plastic zip tie. He was so forceful. The cop used far more force than he needed to. I just lay there on the sidewalk while I listened to the cops take down the queer basher's information. It sucked. I was in pain."

I imagine her hands bound behind her back, her legs tied together, her entire body arched into a taut bow, held immobile on the worn, gum-stained Seattle sidewalk.

"I didn't know what was going to happen next. It was horrifying and exhilarating at the same time. And to this day, all I want to do is take back that night. I want to try on that feeling of helplessness, knowing that I will survive it this time, you know?"

I move to face Jake. I pause. This is serious shit.

"Let me take you there," I say.

Jake carefully runs her fingers through her hair, resting her hand on the back of her head. She shifts her weight. Looks down on the floor before meeting my eyes. She looks straight at me with inquisitive, defiant, yet trusting eyes. She cocks her chin out again, and in a child's voice says, "Okay."

I take a slow but deep breath, check myself, and begin by placing her wrists together behind her back. I carefully wind plenty of rope around them to distribute the pressure. Only a few windings would concentrate it and dig into the wrists much more. Digging in is nice sometimes, because it leaves more pronounced marks afterward, but that's not my goal tonight. Jake stands remarkably still, staring across the room. I notice her breath quickening. She shifts her weight and wriggles her wrists under the rope.

I can't help but stifle a laugh remembering how she was in the bar last night. Today, Jake Six is standing in front of me naked, chin down, submitting.

Then I get nervous. I've asked this girl to trust me. Hogtieing can be tricky. I know I need to get the degree of arch just right.

I used lots of rope to distribute the pressure, right?

Yes, I did.

Okay.

Are you sure about this? I think. *Can I do this?*

Yes.

I can.

I take another slow, controlled breath and then place a hand on her shoulder. "Lie down on your stomach for me."

"Yes, Sir."

I smile to myself, noticing that she suddenly doesn't need the correction anymore.

Shifting her gaze downward, she starts to bend her body to meet the floor. Knees first, she balances on her elbows and crawls down onto her stomach, ass in the air, legs bent at the knees.

"Attaboy. Now for the feet."

I cross her ankles before winding rope around them in the same way as the wrists. After her ankles are cinched down, I run a separate piece of rope up from the ankles, wrapping it around the wrists, then back down to the ankles, making sure the link rope knot is tied at her ankles away from groping fingers.

I silently watch her chest rise and fall. My palms are sweaty.

"Are you ready for me to tighten the rope?"

Jake wriggles her body into a comfortable position on her stomach, breathes deeply, eyes wide before exhaling, "Yes, Sir."

I'm the one supposed to be in control here. I wipe my hands on my jeans and focus.

I double-check all of the ties and slowly pull the link rope just enough so her legs bend, drawing her ankles toward her wrists—creating a living package of helplessness.

"Is that tight enough?"

A second big sigh escapes her mouth. "More, please, Sir."

She's really flexible. I pull the rope tighter, and her crossed ankles cause her knees to spread further apart. "You are such a good boy."

As I am praising her, I'm running my hands all over her body. As I'm touching her, I feel the tension draining from her taut frame. She sinks deeper into the floor. "Feels good, Sir."

"Good. I'm glad. Now, how about we finish what we set out to do when I first arrived here tonight?"

Jake smiles and lets out a laugh. "You are tricky, Sir. There really isn't much I can do about saying no to you, now is there?" Her muscles relax into her own trussed-up body.

"You can always say no, loudmouth."

"Sir," she spits back. "I want you to."

I wrestle my fingers into her hair. "Remind me of what you want."

Smiling, she rolls her eyes in mock exasperation. "Sir, I want you to teach me manners, Sir. Please. Sir."

Her playful willingness gives me the shot in the arm I needed. I kneel behind her so her ankles are at eye level to me. Linking my left hand over her left leg, I open up the cop book again and read the opening pages:

"Becoming a police officer is not for everyone. The most important tenet to being a good officer is the ability to be accommodating to people from all walks of life." I glance down toward her exposed crotch. "Officers must be willing to empathize."

She squirms in position. A restless sigh escapes her.

I put the book down. "Is this boring you?" I say.

"No, Sir. I mean yes, Sir. I mean no, Sir." Her breath is quickening and she's squirming even more now. Her nipples are hard.

"You are practicing restraint, that's good," I say, wriggling her foot and smiling. "Practicing restraint is also a very important tenet of being a good officer."

I trail my hands over her inner thighs, following a path to her clit. Stroking her cunt. "So much restraint." Jake moans while I run my hands down her sides and pull her whole exposed body closer to mine. "Patience too, another good sign."

I unbuckle my jeans and pull out my cock. Jake's rhythmic breath gets me all worked up. I tear my jeans from my body like they are on fire, grab the lube, stroke myself wet a few times, wrap my hands around the underside of her knees, and sink my cock into her.

I start out slowly. Her body pulses with mine. We fuck like a combustion engine, compressed intake stroke cranking her shaft up and down my connecting rod. I arch my back to get a better angle and lube up some more.

She grunts in appreciation. "Sir! Fuck me, Sir!" I rev back up. My piston pumping her intake valve, in and out, faster and faster, building compression, teasing her spark plug. I reach the top of my stroke again as her gasoline charge explodes.

"YES, SIR. YES, Sir. Fuck, yes. Sir." I push in deep, lick my middle finger, and rub her clit with it. "Yes, Sir. Right there."

I feel like I'm doing some kind of yoga pose. Hogtied sutra finger-fuck asana.

The ropes cinch down even further as she comes in my hand. I quickly release the cinch knot. Her body lands in a thud. She lets out a gasp, rolls over on her back. I lie down next to her as we catch our breath.

Jake shoots her head over toward my direction and smiles. I smile back. Then, softly, she asks, "Sir? Are you going to teach me some more manners now or what?"

Baby steps, I remind myself, and laugh.

ALL OF ME

Amelia Thornton

G et down and suck my dick like the filthy little slut you are," I hear myself bark, inwardly cringing at the clichéd dialogue coming out of my mouth. He gets down, though, his own dick straining against the lacy panties I made him put on earlier, the blonde wig he chose himself now all wonky from his exertions. He slobbers all over the black rubber dildo I have strapped on, whimpering about what a sissy slut he is, whilst my mind wanders. It's not that I don't love my job; I do. It's just that towards the end of the day on a Friday, when I've had a whole week of appointments including a regular who flew in from Ohio just to see me, and expected an entire day of Complete Real Life Domination (whatever *that* is), my mind can't help it if it's kind of had enough.

I contemplate dinner to start with. I know you're coming over, and I wanted to do something really special, so I've already been to the market and got all the right ingredients, and the deli to get that walnut bread you love so much, and even managed to find the particular brand of dried mushrooms for the stock that you once told me were the best ones out there. I'm kind of stuck on dessert, but I've still got my next booking to decide that one through, so I guess by the time you pick me up, I'll know what I'm doing.

"Mmmph hmmph hmmph!"

"Yeah, bitch, suck it like that! You like that, huh, such a pretty little cocksucker…"

Okay, so now I'm torn on the lingerie. I know you love the burgundy silk, but you've seen it so many times now. I bought a sheer black babydoll last week that had seemed just perfect at the time, but now I'm thinking it might be a bit too lacy, and you might prefer the simplicity of the silk. Though if I go with the black, I can switch the g-string that came with it for the French knickers with the embroidery trim you always say make my ass look like it's asking for a spanking, which by that point, I'm hoping it will be. So, it's a tough choice.

"Hmmph coming mmph Mistress hhm ohgodyeah…"

I ram the dick a couple times more down his throat whilst he comes, his hand furiously jacking himself off. He always looks a little cute when he comes, this one, like a kind of weird chipmunk with his mouth full of my silicone cock. It's the only way he can come, he told me once, to have something in his mouth. Goes back to his childhood, some older girls making him shove marshmallows in his cheeks til he was nearly sick and they all laughed at him. Hey, I'm not one to judge what gets people off.

"Thank you, Mistress," he whimpers dutifully, reaching for some Kleenex to wipe himself off. "I'll…I'll go and get changed now."

I nod sternly, telling him I'll see him next week for more of the same, and then once he's left the room I slowly start tidying up. I really, really can't be bothered to do another one now. Why

Jackie booked anyone else in is beyond me, when I specifically told her I had a date tonight and didn't want to be late. It's just typical. I'm just in the middle of spritzing all the floggers with sanitizer when I hear the soft click of the door opening and turn around to irritably inform whoever it is that their session doesn't start for another ten minutes, so if they could kindly wait in the waiting room, I will come and fetch them, when I realize it's you.

I can't even speak for a moment, I'm so engrossed in just drinking in the sight of it. You've polished your leathers, and I can smell them from here, that scent of earthy heat I love so much, and you're dressed in it head to toe. Your boots, your jeans, your shirt, your cap: every item gleaming with a dull sheen. Your olive-skinned arms are taut with muscle, accentuated with finely-drawn tattoos, with your fingers hooked in your belt loops the way you know makes me look at your strong, work-worn hands and think about how they feel inside me. Your sharp green eyes, glinting beneath the peak of your cap, are looking at me with the hunger of a woman who knows what is hers and intends to claim it. Just that thought alone makes me wet.

"Wh-what are you doing here?" I manage to stutter, sanitizing the floggers now long forgotten. "Didn't Jackie tell you I've got another appointment?" I can feel the words coming out of my mouth, but I can't really hear them. All I can think of is how good you look, standing right there in front of me in the room where I am not myself. You, who makes me be myself, whether I want to or not.

"'Course she did, babydoll," you reply, your voice smoothly sliding around me, surrounding me. "I booked it."

The sound of your boots against the floor resounds around the room as you slowly, purposefully step towards me. It seems disjointed, you being here in this place where I am *Her*, the "Mistress," this creation that is the opposite of all that I desire but is so much easier to be than the real me. I spend so long building up these walls around me to make me something else, and yet here you are, taking them apart in seconds with just the way you look at me. You stop, just inches from me, your hand reaching out to touch me, your eyes looking into mine with desire and affection and raw, sadistic love. I have spent all day touching, yet there is nothing I want more now than to feel you on me.

Your fingers are tracing imaginary lines on my bare arm, making tiny sparks shoot through my skin, making my breath catch in my throat in anticipation of what you will do to me. I can smell the scent of you, leather and sweat and the musky odor of arousal, and it is filling my head until I can barely stand up, the familiar walls around me seeming wrong, but still familiar. Normally, I have time to get myself out of my workspace head and into my playspace one; go home, take a bath, wash the scent of rubber and baby lotion off my skin; dress for you and only you and wait to feel you take me. Now you are already here, and I am still Her, but it is making my heart pound with need to feel it just as I am.

Slowly, your fingers run through my hair, starting at the roots and dragging out to the very tips, then reaching back up again. It is rhythmic, soothing, but it still puts me on edge. I know you are just toying with me.

"I'm going to tie you up now," you inform me, so calmly and casually you could just be telling me you're off to make a cup of coffee. "I'm going to tie you up, and then I'm going to hurt you. And you're going to thank me for it afterwards. Do you understand?"

I just look at you, my mind snapping back to reality, wondering if I can take this, wondering if this is right, in this situation. All around me are the same black walls I see every day, the mirrors reflecting back the image of me standing next to you, the toys hanging on the walls so much more extreme than anything we would ever play with at home. You'll spank me, and fuck me, and tell me what a good girl I am, but it's not the same, not like this. I'm not like them.

"Do you understand?" Your voice is softer now, your thumb rubbing delicate circles on the inside of my elbow, your fingers gripping my arm gently enough to remind me that they are there, but also to remind me that if you chose to, you could dig deep enough to leave tiny finger-shaped bruises there. I take a deep breath, looking over at my reflection, seeing Her still standing there instead of me.

"Yes, Sir."

You smile, and I know you are proud of me. Your strong hands twist around my wrists, lead me over to the battered leather bench I have used so many times, but never like this. I let you buckle the cuffs around me, feel your hands running over the smooth rubber coating my body, letting myself relax against it, each muscle slowly releasing the tension it has held.

"Don't—don't you want me to take my dress off?" I murmur, thinking momentarily of how much better I would feel naked, exposed and vulnerable before you, ready to feel whatever you wish to inflict upon me. I have my favorite work dress on, the black rubber one with the thick silver two-way zip all the way down the back, the one that's so short I have to wear matching black rubber panties underneath, but at least this means I can still wear my strap-on without too much hassle. I like the way it feels on my skin, clinging and tight and powerful, like a shiny second skin that makes me into Her as soon as I inhale the scent of the latex polish. But you don't seem to want me to stop being Her right now.

Wordlessly, you reach for the zipper, sliding it upwards to reveal the curve of my ass, hooking your fingers into the layer of latex still stretched across my cheeks, rolling down the shining black shorts underneath until I can feel the coldness of the air hitting my skin. The zip is stopped at the small of my back, my entire upper body still encased in the dress, a sheen of perspiration trapped beneath it; I feel safe, wrapped up in rubber, like it is hugging me tightly and not letting go.

"Are you going to be a good girl for me, sugar baby?" you purr in my ear, your fingers back in my hair, running little circles on my scalp. "Are you gonna show me how much you're mine?"

I swallow hard, wondering again if I can do this. Of course I want to be good for you; I always do. It's just that this is so... *alien*.

"What are you going to do to me?" I know answering a question with a question probably isn't going to go down so well, but I try it anyway. You just laugh in response, walking tiny paths of fingertip steps across the exposed flesh of my buttocks, creeping to the line of wetness bisecting me and laughing all the more when you find it.

"I asked you a *question*, little lady. Are you gonna answer me, or am I just going to have to assume from this somewhat conclusive evidence right here"—your thumb slips inside me, just long enough to make me whimper, but not long enough to give me anything else at all—"that you want me to beat your ass red raw till you're screaming for me to fuck you, just to make me stop?"

My stomach flip-flops just at those words, those images, that fleetingly teasing reminder of some part of you inside some part of me. I want you to take me, even if I'm not sure how much you'll take.

"Yes, Sir."

I close my eyes as I hear you walk towards the wall of whips, so attentively cleaned by my own hand. I don't even want to know which one you're going to use, but from the way you softly stroke my skin with it as you walk past, I know exactly which one you've chosen. It's the one I would always pick first myself, the one with the handle made from stainless steel, smooth and curved to fit the grip of its owner, the one with black latex tails curling from it, ready to sting and slice and bring fading darts of red to wherever it lands. I hate how you know me—and you know Her—so well.

I draw in my breath sharply as the thick strands of rubber collide with my bare flesh. It's not that it hurts, as such; more the shock, the sensation of the unexpected, the fact I'm trussed up in my own dungeon without an ounce of control. I screw up my eyes tightly as you bring it back down, wincing as you rain rubberized blows down upon my skin. I want you to stop, sort of; the way that is wanting you to stop in my conscious mind whilst the rest of me insanely wishes for more. You don't stop, of course, just like I knew you wouldn't, but it doesn't stop it feeling strange.

"You like this one, don't you?" It's not so much a question as a statement, really, even though "like" is not exactly the word I would be using right now. If I could speak at all, that is, and I seem to be finding I can't. I mumble some kind of affirmative noise as you slice the sharp strips against the trembling flesh of my thighs, a soft glow spreading across my skin of...what is it, even? Sensation? Painfulness? I can't even tell, but I guess if I was going to verbalize something, it would be something positive. I think so, anyway. You stop briefly, long enough to stroke gentle circles over my reddened cheeks, punctuated with the odd sharp smack of your hand, before striding purposefully back over to the rack of toys.

You must have listened to my inane work chatter more than I thought, as you dutifully lay out the one you have used on the couch next to the sanitizer spray before reaching for another one. I try craning my neck, but even in the reflection I can't see what you're doing, which makes me wriggle just a little in my bonds. Catching me spying, you just chuckle in that way that says "silly little girl," before gritting your teeth and swinging your arm back forcefully, bringing all of your strength down onto me. In my mind, I can see myself propelled forwards, like you are pushing me into a stream of white light, and each strike sends me flying further into it, yet somehow you are still flying next to me. I feel so close to you, it makes me want to tell you then and there how much I love you, but words won't really seem to come out right. You seem to want to make me try, though.

"Are you doing okay, baby?"

"Mmmph-hmmph."

"Is that a yes?"

"Mmm."

"What did I tell you about questions, little missy? You don't want to make me stop now, do you?"

This seems to bring me back to earth somehow.

"No, Sir, please don't stop, Sir. It was a yes, Sir, I'm doing... beautifully, Sir. Th-thank you."

I can almost hear you smiling as I say this. It makes me even happier than I already was. Time seems to pass strangely after that, like an eternity in just a few minutes, where I am certain you use every single thing in that room to inflict blissful agony on me, though how you could have managed it I have no idea. Before I even have time to process it all, your hands are warm on my wrists, tenderly unbuckling the cuffs that bind me, pulling me gently to my feet and into your strong, powerful arms. You hold me there like that, my hammering chest pressed close to yours, like we could just melt into the same person if we stayed there long enough, but I can't stay there long enough. I need you.

"Please let me suck you." I can hear the whisper coming out of my mouth and tiptoeing into your ear, so softly powerful. Whenever I ask you, I know you will let me, but just asking for it sends sparks through me more intense than could ever come from just being ordered to do so.

You take my face in your hands and pull it back to look into my eyes, so full of love for you, and smile.

"Of course you can. Get down on your knees now, that's a good girl."

My gaze does not leave yours as I lower myself to the hard floor, my six-inch work heels bent neatly underneath me, my fingers clinging to your muscular thighs beneath the dull sheen of leather. Your hand tightly grips my hair, forcing my neck back, making me moan so softly in appreciation.

"You gonna show me what a good little cocksucker you are, baby girl?"

I just nod, wide-eyed, my mind filled with the image of your dick rammed down my throat, how hot that makes me, how much I want you. With one hand you unbutton your fly, take out the gleaming length of black silicone I love so much, with the other you start stroking my hair again, in that way that simultaneously arouses and disconcerts me. The blunt tip of your cockhead is so close to my mouth now I could reach out and touch it if I just darted my tongue out, my eyes still fixated on you above me, looking down at your girl. With a gentle nod of your head, you beckon me forward, my painted lips closing around the smooth jet-black surface, pulling back to leave it shining with my spit.

I have tried to understand why it is I love sucking your cock so much. My exes used to freak out about it, tell me it was some kind of patriarchal mind fuck I was into, tell me I should just go get with a guy if that was the kind of weird shit I got off on. I am so glad I don't need to think about that anymore, so glad I can lose myself in the feelings it brings me, knowing you understand it and need it just as much as I do. The way the thickness of the silicone fills up my mouth soothes me somehow, a relaxing expansion against my palate, firm and solid yet still yielding to me, an extension of you that *is* you when you're wearing it, and isn't you as soon as you take it off. It feels somehow primal, to be so lost in something so simple, and I love the way my mind can just go calm as soon as I taste the rubber on my tongue.

But most of all, I love the way you look when I'm doing it. The way your head rolls back just that little bit when I grip the base and grind it into your clit as the tip of it nudges against my throat, stretching the tendons of your neck in a way that makes me want to jump right up there and run my tongue along them. The way you breathe, hard and heavy, your eyes glinting with lust as you watch yourself fuck my mouth, biting your lip as I moan just a little, my eyelids fluttering open and shut as I take just a little more of you than my gag reflex thinks I can. Right now, I can see my reflection in the mirrored walls of my dungeon, my lipstick smeared across my cheeks, hair tangled in your strong fingers, abandoned and passionate and completely devoted to you. I have never felt so beautiful.

"Mmm, that's a good girl," I can hear you murmur, your voice low and throaty, catching just a little as I push that bit harder against your clit. "You look so pretty like this, you know? Giving it up for me. I know you need this, babydoll. I know you need it... Now get that sweet little ass of yours back up on the bench."

I actually whimper as you pull your dick out of my mouth.

Whimper. Man, I would slap some sense into myself if I ever saw me on the street, except for the fact there's quite frankly nothing in the world I want more right now than to feel you inside me, however that is, wherever that is. I know better than to question you, though, even if I do wonder what else there is left in my dungeon for you to hit me with. I obediently get myself back into position, my arms outstretched to feel the leather of the cuffs close around them, but you don't even try to restrain me. You just run your hands protectively over the marks you have just made, almost as if surveying them, admiring them with pride. Then you say those words I have been aching to hear.

"You want it, pretty baby? You want me to fuck you good and hard, now you've been such a good girl for me?"

"Yes, yes, please yes..." My voice is a strangled gasp, desperate and pleading, relieved to at last feel some kind of release for this, the pounding emptiness inside me seeming unbearable now.

"Tell me you want it."

"I want it, I want you, fuck me, please fuck me, my Master..." The words are out of my mouth before I can think of them, before I can check myself and remind myself that I don't use them, remind myself that Masters and Mistresses aren't real, they're just games, games I play all day long. It seems to shock you too, as you fall quiet for just a minute before resting your hands against my hips and pushing the tip of your cock forward until it's nestling against my opening, taunting me with its closeness.

"You're so beautiful right now. My girl." Your voice is soft and gentle, and makes me smile as I lift my head up to look at my reflection in the mirrored wall, my eyes streaked with mascara-drenched tears, you standing behind me, so strong, so authoritative. My Master. Slowly, so slowly, you push yourself inside me, making me bite my lip as a long, low moan curls from my throat, my emptiness filled at last.

I rock my hips back onto you, feeling you going deeper into me, my wetness dribbling out around you, trickling down my thighs and coating the shining silicone with more and more of me. I remember you once told me what you liked most about fisting me was how much wetness came out of me, like I was wrapping you up in the liquid version of myself. I like that image, of me fucking you back as you fuck me, consuming you and absorbing you and bringing you inside myself. I feel like that right now, like we are both all tangled up together, taking and giving and giving and taking, losing ourselves in each other. Looking up at the reflection of me, I see all of the versions of myself looking back, each one so content, right here in this moment. Each one of them is yours, my Master. All of me is yours.

TAKING DIRECTION

Vie La Guerre

I can't take my eyes off you. I watch you sipping, wishing I were a smooth, strong whiskey ginger sliding down your throat, blooming in your belly, making you high. You look at ease, waiting patiently, only looking for me through the crowd every now and then. So simple for you to look cool even though I know you're tensed. I watch your hands. I sit at the horseshoe-shaped bar across from you. I love to watch you so much that I don't order right away; my mind wanders, and I see you check your watch.

"Can I buy you a drink?" In the moment that she asks me, you finally turn your head and catch my eyes. I smile wickedly at you and you see the butch next to me summon the bartender. Good thing you can lip-read "gin and tonic" across the bar. I tear my eyes away from yours and sink them into her, and you know they're liquid and promising as I thank her. Her skin shines caramel and cinnamon, her hair is oily black like her eyes. She's rocking some of that old-school vaquero Mexican style:

embroidered shirt, cowboy boots, needlework everywhere, and smooth Latin lover movements. When she moves her arm, I read her ornate tattoo: Angel.

"Se llama Angel?" I ask sweetly. You see her practiced nonchalant smirk melt for a second from across the room when this blonde femme pronounces her name correctly.

You feel it rising in you as you watch me lean into her and laugh at her jokes. When I incline my head toward her to give her my ear so she can whisper in it, I look at you to make sure you're seeing me. You watch me draw her in. I move my body just right so you know my skirt hikes up my thigh; you can't see but you know from the angle of my body that my garter's showing. That mixture of troubled and turned on is roiling inside you, making you a little harder, a little angry, pulling that tension in your body until you see me lean in and reach my hand around her head. The second you see my short, dark nails touch her neck, you're up and moving.

"Hi." Your voice is tight and in an instant, everything's obvious.

Angel looks between us and then decides to start with you: "Can I help you, man?" I smile at you under my skin, just a touch of mirth, and you can feel my heat as you put your hand on my shoulder.

"Well," you start, weighing how far you're willing to go, "yeah, you probably can. Here's the thing with this femme of mine." You look me up and down, your gaze appraising, proprietary. You step over to talk to Angel. I'm out of hearing range now but I've done my part, so I'm waiting, watching, seeing how much bait you're going to take.

"Come on." You grab my upper arm and pull me up out of my seat. You steer me firmly toward the door and I'm momentarily disappointed. Then I see Angel following not far behind, and a flash of heat hits me and my cunt starts dripping. My high heels hit the floor steadily as I saunter, keeping my pace just slow enough that you have to pull me along. When we get to the alley, the cold air breathes relief around me and I smell the salt-tinged night fog start to fall.

"Stand here." You spin me facing you and push me against the cold brick wall. The throbbing music inside comes through the mortar and touches my pulsing, steaming skin.

Angel strolls up, looks me up and down as I lean, breathless, shoulders on the wall. "So," she says to you. "She's yours, but she likes to hit on other guys, is that right?"

You raise your chin in a short backwards nod. "Yeah, seems that way." I dart my eyes between you, unsure what's going to happen but hoping, straining against my rising fear, the desire to break the spell and start running.

You look directly at me. "So, I think she needs a lesson in how to behave. You wanna help me teach her, man?" Angel looks me up and down and licks her lips. The red embroidered roses on her black button-up look like they're dripping, bleeding, soaking everything around them, and I feel moisture running down my thighs. You pull your joint out of your vest pocket and light it, dragging off it slowly. You raise your eyebrows and extend your hand to Angel, who takes a hit.

"Why don't you see how excited it makes her to go out without me and get other guys' attention?" you say to Angel. She steps toward me and grabs my waist, keeps one hand there as she brings the other to my neck and sweeps my hair out of the way.

"She's got goose bumps," Angel reports from right up close so I can feel her hot breath on my ear.

"Slut," you say languidly. "Her nipples are probably hard, too." Angel's right hand moves deftly over my collarbone, down my neckline. She reaches into my low-cut dress and rubs her fingers gently over my bra.

"I dunno, man, it's hard to tell through her bra, you know?" Angel says.

"Well, take one of her tits out, then. She won't care, she's been showing herself off to everyone. What's one more rough night in an alley, right, babe?" Your voice is sure enough that Angel takes your direction. Your tone has that challenge for me in it: How long can I take it? How long can I trust you and let you play with me this way, just a big, expensive toy that you show off?

Angel slides her smooth right hand down my chest and into the cup of my bra. She pulls the weight of my breast up and my strap slides down my shoulder at the same time, so the front of my dress falls and allows you to see my white skin and pink nipple completely bare. The cold air hits my goose-bumped skin and I almost moan because of the throbbing in my cunt. Angel circles my nipple with her thumb.

"Yeah, her nipple's hard. She's turned on, man. This girl is begging for it." You exhale a puff of smoke. My head lolls back against the wall; I'm trying desperately not to scream. Trying to keep it together as her practiced thumb teases my cold, hard nipple.

"Yeah, she's in heat." You shrug. "She's always like that. I'll bet her pussy's slick and the tops of those stockings are soaked, too. You should find out."

Angel's hand remains on my nipple and I think for a second she's lost her nerve. Then I remember she has another hand, as I feel her left slide down my body and run up my stocking-covered thigh. I shudder as her hand slides from my outer thigh to the inside, where my legs are touching.

"Shit, she's so hot I can feel her before I even get close," Angel tells you.

"Baby," you say. I look into your eyes. "Baby, spread your legs. Let her see how much it turns you on to get everyone's attention." I move my foot to the side so that my legs make an A shape.

"Haha, man, she moved and it all fell into my hand. You weren't kidding. This girl is so, so wet."

"I know," you say, looking right at me, mocking. "She's got a sweet pussy, too. You should feel her."

Angel looks right at me and smiles. "Mmm, baby. You got a sweet little pussy for me, huh? I know it's sweet 'cause I've been smelling you all night. You want me to touch it?" I am practically ready to drop my weight into Angel's strong, sure hand, I'm so desperate for some friction. You look at me, warning me not to speak. I plead with my eyes and keep silent.

"Touch her, she can take it," you say. Angel moves her hand slowly and rubs my vulva with the lips still closed, letting all my wet, silky skin run over itself and sending shards of sharp wanting up my spine. She taps my closed pussy just hard enough, and I gasp. Her fingers part my lips and run up and down all of my sensitive folds, and her thumb keeps circling my nipple until her first finger joins it. She pinches hard and her fingers slide inside me. Two, then three she thrusts and I open easily, throbbing, soaking her hand to the wrist. She looks up at me, bright-eyed, and suddenly her bravado is mostly gone except for that little bit that laces her naked lust.

I'm watching you as she's pinning me to the wall with the hand that's on my breast. Your cheeks are flushed and you've begun rubbing your cock absently, watching my pupils dilate and my mouth chew my lips together in order to keep quiet. You read my face and know her hand is working me over, that I'm so turned on and so close that I need a shuddering orgasm or three to relieve all this tension. As Angel thrusts into me, your eyes never leave mine.

I'm starting to ride Angel's hand hard now, waiting, wanting to come, needing my release, needing it to rip through my clamped throat and tight muscles.

Your voice is low, controlled, but loud enough to break the spell. "So what do you think?"

Angel steps back, disengages from me. Her face changes as she returns to herself, collecting her machismo and spreading it back over her face. Smirk. She brings her hand to her mouth. "Yeah, man," she says, her breath measured, with effort. "Sweet girl you have here." I'm throbbing, wanting to grab her hand and force it back to my cunt, needing to come with all my body's force.

"Make her clean your hand for you," you say. Angel brings her hand close to my mouth and I suck my taste off her fingers, one by one, acidic and sweet, sharp and salty. The taste of your mouth when you've made me scream, the taste of my own fingers when I've been coming all night long alone thinking of you. Angel pulls her hand away and offers you her right hand from my breast. You shake it, and the two of you seem to share a little self-satisfied moment of butchy brotherly affection as I pull my dress back up. When I lift my head, she's gone. You step heavily closer to me and grab my hair, kiss me hard.

I start to whimper, "Baby, make me come, I need to come, please baby why you tease me like that, please..." You back up.

"I know you want to come, baby. Maybe later." You take my upper arm and lead me to the car. You bend your head after I'm seated in the passenger side and grab my pussy as I fasten my seat belt. Your breath is hot on my ear, and full of growl and promise: "Let's get you home."

BLACK HANKY

Sassafras Lowry

Hy left the femmes at the club and took me home instead. The decision surprised hym a whole lot more than it did me. See, hy was raised up a Southern gentlemanly sort of butch. The kind of butch that opened doors, buys dinner, and always brings flowers on a date. The sort of butch who was looking for a wife who would make sure hy had a cold glass of sweet tea waiting when hy got home from work. Hy didn't bring me flowers. I wasn't going to be anyone's wife.

We made our escape while the girls were in the bathroom and drove in silence. I'd played with other tops before. Butches I'd puppy-dog followed out of social justice and political meetings. They were northern city butches with silicone cocks and floggers made from expensive leather. Butches with St. Andrew's Crosses in their basements and eye bolts in the ceiling. Hy was different, rougher. Here there was no posturing or pageantry, just connection, just sex, just power.

We went into hys darkened house and passed the closed doors

of hys roommates. I was grateful for the privilege of avoiding small talk. Hy closed the door behind us and clicked on the exposed bulb. I tried to take in my surroundings, the cardboard movie cutout of James Dean, the signed Indigo Girls posters, but I felt boot meet flesh and my knees buckled, leaving me on the floor in front of hym. Black hanky swiftly pulled from my back right pocket and the room plunged into darkness. "You think you have a right to flag black, boi? We'll see about that."

My knees buckled, mind flooding with playback videos of all the times I'd pushed past my breaking point as a high school athlete. The physical therapy that restored full range of motion but could only do so much. My knees are no longer designed for kneeling, but I wanted to give hym this. Pushed past the edge of pain, the stabbing pain transitioned to hot burning. Pushing past the pain would be worth it for one head pat, for one "good boi."

No sooner had I settled into the burn of my knees than I felt hys boot at my back, pushing me forward face first into the dirty bedroom carpet. The synthetic fibers scratched my face and did little to cushion the blow as I collided with the floor. Still blindfolded, I forced my breathing to quiet so I could listen for hym, trying and failing to anticipate where hys next move would come from. My hands were ripped from where they casually lay at my sides behind my back and cinched tight with rope, boot still pressed firmly into my spine. I knew the clean work shirt I'd chosen for the occasion of going out tonight now bore the outline of hys muddy right boot. Thoughts of when I'd next be able to do laundry left my mind as hy scruffed me, fingers digging into the short hairs at the back of my neck, pulling me back to my knees.

Hys breath hot on my face, I was pulled into a rough bruise of a kiss my lips would feel for days. Hys hands slipped flat-palmed down across my chest. Caught between pushing into hym and pulling away, I held my breath as hy with frightening gentleness undid shirt buttons, untucked my undershirt, and reached beneath. Hys lips again found me as hy pulled me to hym and undid the Ace bandage holding my chest down. I wanted to protest but didn't want this to end. Hy grabbed my left nipple hard as I heard the metallic unzipping of hys fly, and my jaw was forced to make room for hys delicious cock.

"What do you say, boi?"

"Thank you."

"Thank you, *what*?"

"Thank you, Daddy!"

"Good boi."

Smiling around hys cock, I stuffed back a giggle of amusement that we'd both hard-packed tonight. For a butch who said hy never fagged, hy sure seemed into this. I thought of making a smart comment to that effect but could already feel the red welt of a palm against my face and thought better of the insubordination fantasy.

Grabbing my shirt collar, hy pulled me up onto hys unmade bed. Hys other hand fumbled with my belt buckle and zipper. I was left stripped of pants and boxers, with only my harness and boots left as armor. Nakedness feeling all the more profound as I felt hym press into me, binder and shirt intact, cock protruding through the fly of hys jeans. Hy bit my shoulders and I bucked up against hym, reaching out in blindfolded darkness. I wanted to wrestle, wanted to fight, but I was so deep into this I could make little more than a feeble attempt.

Hy was on top of me now, pushing me into the mattress and kneading the tense muscles in my back. I must have relaxed slightly because soon hys hand was under me, grabbing my cock and beginning to stroke, finding me hard and wet for hym. Hys other hand moved the middle strap of my harness aside and pushed hys cock in hard. I gasped and hy whispered that I better be grateful and keep quiet. Hy fucked me harder, pulled my hand down to my own cock, and I began stroking. Hy was using my harness as a handle for better leverage, getting deeper and moaning through clenched teeth with each thrust. With each thrust hy went deeper than was comfortable. My resolve broke, throat erupting in a stream of moans and "please" and "Daddy, don't stop."

I found my coordination and was able to stroke myself in time to each thrust. I was so close, right on the edge, when hy paused. For a moment I thought hy was stopping, that this was a cruel tease, but then hy pushed in deeper than before with a growl, shudder, and moan that told me hy'd just finished in me. Hys final thrust and moan sent me over the edge and I began coming around hys cock, in my hand, shuddering beneath hym.

We lay together for a few minutes, panting. I felt the sweat run off hys forearms onto my back and the sticky warmth of hys shirt against my ass. I opened my eyes and discovered that at some point the blindfold had come off; the room was disheveled and poorly lit. I rolled over and kissed hym deeply when I heard a buzzing beside my head. Hys phone, dropped earlier on the nightstand, was vibrating. Rolling off me, hy picked it up and scrolled through a text message.

"The girls are wondering where we went, I better get back," hy muttered, tucking hys cock back into hys jeans and running a comb through hys hair. I scrambled to pull on my pants, not believing that after all this hy was going back to the club, going back for the femmes we'd ditched earlier. Hy tactfully went to the bathroom to give me time to bind again. When hy returned, I was sitting on the edge of hys bed.

"I'm ready to go," I said, trying to keep my voice from trembling.

"Not quite," hy growled, pressing my black hanky into my hand. "You earned this, boi," he said, and then motioned I should follow hym back through the dark house and out to hys truck.

SPANKING BOOTH

Dusty Horn

I f you think all it takes to run a successful sexy fund-raiser is a good-looking person under a sign that says 'Kinky Kissing Booth,' you are sorely mistaken." My colleague Lisa grins, gently guiding a little blonde thing off my lap and handing him a glass of water.

Lisa is a bombshell high-femme transsexual, 6'2" in stilettos, and thus the perfect maternal figure for endorphin-befuddled spankees.

"How do you pull it off so well?" this satisfied customer asks dreamily, pulling his rubber skirt down with some effort and rubbing the smarting bottom beneath.

I field this one. I am feeling quite pleased with myself and perhaps a little top-drunk at all the fresh, no-strings-attached meat this gig gets me.

"A spanking booth requires a hustler of the highest order, preferably a team of slick hustlers with a relaxed but firm hierarchy of command."

It's 1:15 a.m. on a Saturday night, and I am running one such well-oiled machine at a leather destination in the SOMA district of San Francisco. I've assembled a half dozen foxy tops plus a few delectable switches and bottoms of varying genders to appeal to every conceivable unassuming queer to darken the doors of the bar tonight.

"It's just like flirting," I continue pontificating to no one in particular. "You have to be available without coming on too strong. You have to make the bottom think it was their idea all along."

We are raising money for some sex-positive organization; I can't remember if they even told me which one it is this time. Regardless, if there are two skills I am happy to volunteer for the cause of my community, it's my superb kinky talents and my capacity to work a crowded room.

My cohorts and I have had a wildly successful night, of course. We offer penetrating kisses, ruthless tit torture, face slapping, verbal humiliation, and for the more adventurous, flogging, caning, and strap-on sucking.

Although I delight in dishing out all of these activities, my personal specialty is spanking.

I am sitting in the room's place of power—the James Bond seat, I like to call it. From this chair, I can clock the movements and motivations of everyone in the room while keeping my back up against the wall. No one surprises me, and I keep an eye on everyone who is even considering working up the courage to approach us and ask for what they need.

My leather pants are skintight but comfortable, and my white tank top clings to my torso with just the right amount of sweaty exertion. Many people think of soiled boots as sacrilege, but mine stomp too much dirt, kick too much shit to stay clean for long. When you see me filthy, you know I mean it.

While others devote time to moisturizing their leather, I have my hands full beating twice as much ass. But hey, there's no accounting for taste.

Speaking of taste, from my vantage point I can see a clutch of tacky little twinks causing a commotion.

"What do you think that ruckus is about?" asks my colleague Jeremy, a barrel-chested bear who will tweak your nipples like it's going out of style.

"Based on the time of night..."

"Morning!" he corrects me with a grin and wet-lipped swig of foamy beer.

"Duly noted. The time of morning and the pitch of their squawks makes me think: peer pressure."

"No doubt." We laugh together.

Our laughter turns to wry amusement when the boys drag over the object of their pressure, and it turns out to be:

A very sexy, very ambivalent-looking tough girl.

Years of experience have given me a good sense of whether butch or femme presentation indicates a cisgendered, transgendered, or genderqueer person. Not that it makes any particular difference to me; we all have asses, after all.

From this femme's lack of Adam's apple, and her apparent fag-haggery, I would peg her for the pussy-having variety.

Of course, I am never unhappy to be proven wrong.

Her faggot friends have all the attractive attributes of well-trained dolphins. They are sharp and sleek, but also eager to please and susceptible to suggestion.

"We have a client for you!" the queeniest of them sings.

Tough Girl and I size each other up.

She is wearing jeans so skinny they are practically tights, a black bustier, and an oversized leather jacket. It's the perfect combination of "Look at me!" and "Fuck you for looking at me!" Her eyeliner and hair have seen the effects of the evening.

"Don't you feel bad about taking the hard-earned money of drunken queers?" she sneers.

"No," I answer levelly. I have been asked this question before. "If I wasn't the recipient, then the bar, or the corner store, or the man selling onion-stuffed bacon-wrapped sausages on the street would be."

She stands slack-jawed. Perhaps she is used to being the intimidator with little resistance. Perhaps it has made her soft.

I actually offer her quite a chance to think of a clever reply before sipping my scotch and continuing.

"If there's one thing I've learned from years of hustling, it's that people enjoy parting with their money even more than they enjoy earning it. They don't care *where* it's going as long as they feel satisfied in the moment that there is an equal exchange of quality and quantity. It gives them a perverse sense of losing control."

"What this bitch needs is a good spanking!" Queenie mercifully interrupts me, shutting my mouth by producing a bill.

"Well! Giving people a perverse sense of losing control is my trade, actually. And if people are gonna throw money at a vacuum, I might as well be there with a trash bag to catch the discarded pieces of paper."

I nod at Jeremy, who relieves the boy of his cash in a way that already makes him feel it was well spent.

"What is your name?" I ask Tough Girl.

The boys try to be helpful.

"Beth!" they sing.

"I am going to *murder* all of you!" she sneers with clenched fists. Yet no one is holding her there. She does not stomp for the door.

"Beth," I ask, "would you like to be spanked?"

She whirls back to face me, crossing her arms over her ample chest.

"Yeah, I guess so, why not?"

"Good. Consent is very sexy. Now. You think that because this is your friends' idea, you are absolved of the stigma of your desire."

Our eyes are locked now.

"You are not fooling me, oh no. I knows desire when I sees it."

I have a bench arranged for the dabblers, the people who want the sensation of being spanked but are neither prepared nor inclined toward the deeper humiliation or fantasy subsumation of a true OTK. For that latter purpose, however, I have appropriated one of the bar's armless chairs.

Honestly, why chairs ever have arms on them is beyond me.

I take Beth's left hand and stare up at her. My knees are crossed, and I am turned ever so slightly to my right to face her. Ordinarily the power dynamics are best realized when the sadist places herself above the masochist. However, when you have cultivated palpable dominance, it is even preferable to be in an unexpected position. It throws them off, says all bets are off.

"Have you ever been spanked before?" I ask with the dispassionate curiosity of a tattoo artist about to give an eighteen-year-old her first tramp stamp.

"No!" she snorts, breaking eye contact.

See what I mean? She could be twice my size and I would still tower over her.

"Liar! Slut! Harlot!" comes the protestation of her entourage.

"Is this true?" I uncross my leg coolly. I guide her body slowly down to my level, holding her fast with my eyes and my firm grasp, until she is squatting.

"Are you lying to me?"

Beth squirms.

"I...I mean...I've been spanked, during...you know..."

"Sex?"

The follies shriek, fluttering their black and neon fingernails. "Doggy style!" they offer.

"No, no, she's talking about when she takes it in the *butt!*"

"I do *not* take it—" Beth begins to stand, to turn her head in protest.

"Beth," I coo. "Pay them no mind."

She turns her eyes slowly back to mine.

"Do you get off on pain?"

"Yes," she answers without hesitation. Then after a pause, "Why did I tell you that?"

"I have a good ability to get the truth out of people," I reply. We stare at each other.

I got a live one! I think. The room is thinking the same thing, no doubt.

"You will stop being defiant now. You will address me as Ma'am. You will only speak when spoken to unless it is to use your safeword. Your safewords are yellow and red. Are you familiar with the meaning of those colors?"

"Yeah, like a traffic light, right? I get it."

Before she can blink, I have her by the hair at the nape of the neck with my left hand. I pull her across me, expertly guiding the seat of her pants over my lap.

She makes a delightful noise of abandon, something like, "Whaaaarpm!"

I apply a dozen healthy hard spanks to the outside of her jeans as her black-and-white sneakers kick indignantly in the air.

"I get it *what*?" I inquire firmly.

"Wu-what?"

Firing off another dozen punitive smacks, knowing they aren't doing much damage besides getting my point across, I consider what an excellent method a pants-on spanking is for forming denim to a body.

"She wants you to call her ma'am," a helpful friend chimes in.

Disoriented and flustered, Beth acquiesces.

"Oh! Jesus Christ. Yes *ma'am*."

"Good girl! Now we're getting somewhere." I massage my damage. This admission of authority always puts me in a cheery mood.

"Let's get a look at how you've colored from those initial spanks."

I begin to pull down her jeans, and she throws her hands back to hold them in place.

"It's not okay that I take your pants down?" I ask with genuine respect.

"N-no! I want you to. It's just that…"

"What is it, girl?"

"I didn't know anyone would be seeing my panties tonight. Tomorrow is laundry day, and these are my *boring* panties."

I throw my head up and laugh uproariously.

"Don't you know it's not your panties I want? It's what's inside them," I declare as I unbuckle her brown leather belt and start to work the jeans over her hips. It's easier said than done.

"Honestly, I think this trend of skintight jeans was invented to infuriate tops," Lisa cracks, for the benefit of the rowdy room.

The denizens of the bar are watching with increased interest.

Beth assists me on more than one level by wriggling out of her pants. It is a truly delicious ass that pops, liberated, to attention. She wasn't kidding; her underwear is cotton, formerly white, washer-worn. But it just makes me feel more like I am imposing my will on something that wasn't expecting me.

I like this feeling.

I will spank anyone who wants a spanking from me. But it takes the right kind of ass for me to enjoy myself, to awaken the sadist in me.

Tonight's my lucky night.

I bend over slightly and hiss in her ear. "I haven't had an ass this fine across my lap in a while, girl."

She murmurs gleefully. I haven't met a bottom yet who doesn't love to be praised, even the ones who crave humiliation.

The warmup for a spanking sounds like an orchestra tuning up in an empty cavernous concert hall. It smells like a teenage football team stretching in the locker room before the big homecoming game. Soon there will be a harmonic cacophony, expertly executed strategic force.

For those of us in it for the long haul, we must prepare ourselves.

Without her denim to pad the blows, every touch of my hand speaks to Beth more clearly. Still, her panties soak up the sting. She feels much more exposed than when her pants protected her, but she still has a fortress of cotton between her precious skin and my advancing forces.

Balanced tenuously between mortification at her present exposure and relief at this last vestige of dignity that is her panties, Beth is slowly becoming mine.

I start to lull her into more complacency with a steady rhythm and intensity. First one cheek, then the other gets two loose flicks of my wrist. The first is a momentary massage, followed closely by a solid thwack. She has just enough time to experience pain in one cheek before her attention is redirected to the soothing touch on the other. She is getting about thirty smacks and thirty rubs per minute, a nice droning pace designed to isolate both of us from the bar's stimulation.

"Are you ready for your panties to come down?"

Our cunts are very close together, if a bit askew, and our evident mutual enjoyment is generating quite a lot of heat. We both feel it, and our sympathy for one another grows. Through the sleek leather of my pants I sense her relaxing, allowing herself to be held and used and guided. She senses my control, and trusts me.

"Yes ma'am."

I make a big show for my growing audience of peeling the panties down, leaving them just below the cheeks to frame her luscious pinkness.

"Aaaand they're off!" Lisa narrates, producing a cheer from the crowd.

I take great mounds of her ass in both hands and squeeze the flesh like I am prepping some precious material for some obscure art project. Released, these handfuls bounce back into place, vibrating ever so slightly as they settle.

I am meticulous about covering all my territory. I set about creating a symmetrical coloration for my visual pleasure and even sensation for hers.

"There is a target on every ass," I narrate for my captivated voyeurs. "Right here." I trace three concentric circles in the middle of each cheek, punctuating them with a bull's-eye smack that makes my victim howl and the audience cheer.

"But the ass has so much more to offer. You have to spread the blood around..." I demonstrate rapid tapping around the side of each cheek and play the cleavage of her heart shape like perfect bongo drums.

"And of course there's the tender insides. You have to be prudent here; it's much more sensitive, especially when they are aroused..."

"I am *not* turned on by this!" Beth protests, arching her back.

My hand reacts instinctively to bratty behavior such as this. It snakes between her legs and pries them open, landing five perfectly placed windmill blows at a difficult angle: the sideways curve of the lady's ass into her cunt.

She squeals but before she knows what is happening, the pain and vulnerability of this recourse has subdued her further. Then she merely melts and whimpers.

"This inner spot is for punishing insolent behavior and reinforcing roles."

The crowd laps it up. Queers do so love a good drama.

I stroke the pinkening skin and raise goose bumps down her back with the fingernails of my non-opposable hand.

"Jeremy, will you oblige me?" Without taking my eyes off my prize, I indicate the crumpled pants on the ground.

Knowing exactly what I have in mind, Jeremy whistles through his teeth and stoops to extract Beth's belt from its loops. He does it quickly, demonstrating the belt's whip-like potential. Always a showman, he folds it in half and produces a satisfying crack that strikes fear and lust into the heart of every bottom in the room.

"I find it extra humiliating to be beaten with one's own belt," I say as Jeremy hands me Beth's.

This little distraction snaps her out of her complacency somewhat. She begins to squirm.

"Now, when I send you home you will wear the weapon I used against you. Every time you wrap it around your waist, you will think of its potential. And you will think of me."

I hold the buckle in my palm and wrap the leather slowly around my hand, familiarizing myself with its weight and texture. When only about a foot's length is left, I hold out my other hand and test its strength on my forearm.

It bites like a bitch, leaving a red tab on my skin.

"Are you ready to taste your own belt, little girl?" I ask, teasing her with the soft flap, the result of the leather molding to the appropriate loop of that sexy waist.

"Yes please, ma'am," she squeaks.

As the blood rushes to Beth's cheeks, so the blood rushes more palpably through my heart as I bring the belt down hard on her ass. My head rushes and my cunt throbs. The darkening of the soft pink to a dark red is visible even in the low bar light. I paint her entire ass this color, covering as much ground as possible before doubling back. When the belt retreads over already visited territory, it leaves a ghostly white mark before the red fills in.

Beth does not struggle anymore. After the slow seductive warmup, the belt controls her utterly.

I unleash myself on the bottom that now yearns for more. Soon my blows are both hard and quick. The belt grows from my hand, from my desire, and from hers.

Soon the shrill queens, the hard rock music, the reek of stale booze fade away, and so does every part of her body that isn't over my lap. There is only my belt and her ass. It has only ever been this way, like the waves crashing on the beach. Our play is a force of nature.

I'm sure she could have taken it forever. But the bartender hollers that fatal cry:

"Last call for alcohol!"

The room comes rushing back, noises and smells first. I uncoil the belt and rapidly rub her ass with it like I am shining a bowling ball. Tossing my instrument on the ground next to the crumpled pants, I proceed to softly stroke her sore bottom.

To my delight, my aftercare elicits sweet murmurs and undulations. We breathe and contract together, grinding and grounding one another.

My hands snake through the hair at the nape of her neck again.

"You are going to stand up. Slowly, and you are going to keep your head down so the blood doesn't rush to your head."

"Yes ma'am."

"Good girl. If you're gonna faint on me, it'll be from pain, not sloppiness."

She gulps visibly. "Yes ma'am."

Soon Beth is standing, a happy pulverized mess. I stand too and put my arm around her quivering body.

"May I buy you a drink, my good little girl?"

She nods slowly, gazing at me like she is seeing me for the first time.

"Later this week, with some of the money we earned at the spanking booth, I'll buy you dinner."

THE CRUELEST
KIND

Kiki DeLovely

Half leading, half dragging me out the back door of the club, She kicks the door exiting into the alleyway and slams me up against the brick wall. Cool against my flushed face for a second, then a flash of hot as She gets too rough with that fistful of hair, scraping my cheek against the prickly texture.

"What the fuck did you think you were doing in there?"

I know there's no correct response, so I just wait. Calmly. Let Her blood boil just a bit more.

"You little fucking cocktease! You think that's how it's going to be?"

I feel just the faintest trickle of blood run down my face and think for a moment it's the sweat I worked up on the dance floor. As I'm about to wipe it away, it hits me that it's blood and I'm glad I realized this just in time. In time to leave it there. She'll like that. And I think back on the events of the evening leading up to this moment... Dancing around all the butches in the club, letting Her dip me here and there, flirting brazenly with Her buddies, twirling away from Her hands whenever they inched too far up my skirt, and once—just once—taking that hand and sliding Her fingertips through my wetness. (There are definite advantages to my occasional no-panty-wearing ways.) Then walking away. To flirt with the most imminent form of trouble: Her best friend.

Just as I approached that danger (the surest type of danger) and smiled (that smile)—not even long enough to bat an eyelash—I felt my head snap back as She helped Herself to a fistful of my hair and locked an uncomfortably firm grip on my wrist, twisting it behind my back. Suddenly I was in the alley. Against this brick wall. Slightly out of breath in anticipation. Knowingly deserving of every second of what's to come.

"That's not how it's going to be—I'll show you how it's going to be." And just as I feel Her gearing up to demonstrate just what's in store for me, we're blinded by headlights and She whips me around, growling in my ear, "Kiss me. And make it look good." Her tongue plunges so quickly into my mouth it takes me a second to catch up, match Her motions, and snake one leg up around Her. After the car passes, She's back at my ear, hissing, "We don't want anyone calling the cops on some little slut getting raped in the back alley. Especially when I haven't even started yet."

And with that I decide to take the game to a whole new level. I slap Her across the face and take off running, further down into the darkness. It's not as if I was going to get very far in those heels anyway. Four and a half additional inches added to my already Amazonian stature, the extra elevation dizzies me whenever I falter. The heels She told me to wear tonight. The heels that I'll only wear for Her. And inevitably regret it the next day.

She catches me in less than ten paces, hurling me up against a chain-link fence. "You stupid little cunt, did you really think you could get away?" She grabs that same fistful of hair, yanking it back far enough away to slap me back—harder—then pushes my face back into the metal. She kicks my legs apart, spreading them as far as they will go and still keep some semblance of balance in those heels. Pressing Her stiff dick up against my ass (I can feel Her hardness through Her jeans—I love it when She packs hard), grinding into me even more forcefully, Her fingers form the beginnings of bruises on my hips as they hold me in a death grip. The chain link cutting into bits of my exposed flesh, my fingers clenched through the holes, I'm hopelessly pinned there. Her strength and weight crushing against me. I'm completely at Her disposal. Just how She likes it. The suffering I incur from this humility pains me much greater than anything physical She's doled out yet tonight. A deliciously difficult position. And one I know won't last for long.

She lets up just enough to reach down, and before I even know what's happening, shoves Her fingers (how many I'm not exactly sure, at least two, no more than four) deeply into my dripping hole and I can't help but cry out.

"This. This is mine. Along with everything else under that pretty little skirt of yours. I'll take whatever I want. Whenever I want. And do with it as I please." She pulls out and turns me around so that I can look into Her eyes, witness the intent behind them, while She begins to undo just the middle two buttons of Her jeans. I glare back disobediently and so She slaps me across the face—the sting of it biting especially well on my raw, scraped-up cheek. My hand instinctively flies through the air to return the favor, but She's too quick, anticipating this, and catches me by the wrist. She holds it there, midair, tightly enough to cut off my circulation for a few seconds (seconds that feel like minutes, my gaze locked hard, defiantly, the entire time), while She continues to work Her fly slowly, deliberately. Then, out of nowhere, She's dragging me even further down the alley. I can barely keep up, let alone see where She's taking me, as I stumble along and try to keep from falling. No more sweet formalities, She throws me over the side of Her motorcycle and begins to whale on my exposed ass. The blows keep coming, each one harder and faster than the one before. Clearly, there will be no warming up tonight. Even with the sinking of my teeth into my lips, I can only take it briefly before the shrieking betrays me.

She either grows impatient or doesn't want to chance it with the cops and so She stops just long enough for me to catch half a breath and to roll on a condom before She thrusts Her cock into my cunt so fast I cry out again. A different kind of cry this time—one that tells a story, for those who are in the know—that of a little less pain, slightly more pleasure. I feel Her dick pump brusquely in and out of me a few times and then...nothing, my pussy left wanting, practically begging for more as a whimper escapes me and I begin to squirm against the bike. I can almost feel the corners of Her lips curling up, happy to have left me so vulnerable and needy that it hurts. This makes my need to squirm all the greater, so I attempt to push myself up, pull myself together, anything, to regain a sliver of dignity. Then, without warning, I suddenly stop. Call it female intuition. Or perhaps more like survival instinct. I just know.

"You know what you're gonna do?" She asks slowly, a particular flavor of serenity in Her voice. One could almost mistake it for sweetness. That is, if one didn't know any better. Her tone, cadence, even Her energy have completely shifted in these brief moments, and the calm of it all leaves me frozen in midair. She has regained a firm, undeniable upper hand. "You're going to press your palms up against that brick wall in front of you and you're not going to move a single, solitary muscle, not an inch, not even one millimeter."

Mental bondage. The cruelest kind. A kindness and a cruelty twisted together into a sick, sadistic love child. Sure, I love to struggle, fight back, purposely act out, and behave inappropriately. I daydream for hours on end, plotting new and creative ways to fuck with Her head, wanting to earn every blissful moment of agony and ecstasy. But disobey a direct command? I simply cannot. And She knows this. Tether me to a pole and whip me relentlessly—I can writhe around uncontrollably, my body flailing violently with very little repercussion, rejoicing in my tremulous dance. Here I must display complete control with every breath, cautious not to neglect for even half a second that I am utterly confined by invisible shackles. The ultimate subjugation. This. This intellectual and physical mind fuck. This is what torture is really all about. The pain is in my head, the pleasure in my body. And when one becomes too much to handle, they switch places.

She stands back for a minute to watch it all sink in. Satisfied but not yet sated, She decides I haven't experienced sufficient humiliation and degradation, so She bends me over further still. Meticulously following Her orders, I'm careful to only move of Her volition; the palms of my hands scrape against the brick as She poses me exactly to Her liking. The cerebral hold She's got on me far from necessitates any physical assistance, but it pleases Her to leave me as exposed, tormented, and defenseless as possible. So She uncoils a length of thinly gauged crimson red rope from Her saddle bag and kicks my legs apart. It is even more challenging to obey now that I have been deprived of practically any sense of balance; my body wants to give out, but my arrogant nature can only be characterized as quite the determined little brat who never backs down. So I steel my perseverance on the inhale, revel in my suffering on the exhale.

Working swiftly and skillfully, it's only a matter of minutes before She has my pussy splayed and expertly displayed for any passerby to savor and the cool chill in the air to ravish. The rope is secured tightly across my most sensitive bits of flesh, purposefully, so that when I quiver slightly, I gasp for air. Should I twist my hips, I'd be brought to my knees. Even the simple act of breathing is cause for Her tethers to grate against my lips. The abrasions are sure to last for quite some time. I take great pride in knowing this. Withstanding the pull and burn, delighting in marks that act as trophies, I'll be cherishing the pain that lingers and heals over in the weeks to come.

Amused by Her handiwork, She steps back again, admiring the view. Making me wait. Listening to my ragged breath. She waits just one more beat before returning, dick in hand, and drives into Her gaping, glistening prize. I try to keep quiet and not let on just how much I need this, but She can sense my titillation. Deciding She's taking it too easy on me, She denies me this indulgence as quickly as She granted it, pulls out of my pussy, and a split second later is pressing the head of Her slick cock up against my asshole.

"You enjoyed yourself a little too much there, didn't you? Spread so wide, I could practically shove my fist in too and jack myself off inside your cunt. Well, now you're going to take it where I want it, you filthy fuckin' whore. Every last inch of me. So you better open up." Adding, just before She slams into me, "You're allowed to fight me now, but just know that I'll win. I'm not afraid to make my own hole."

GOING THE DISTANCE

Elaine Miller

It was a Saturday night. I've got a thing for being exactly on time. I know it's unreasonable, but I secretly wish everyone else felt the same. Maria said she'd pick me up at ten, and there I was at five minutes past, surreptitiously taking off my leather jacket and slinging it over a chair so I wouldn't look quite so obsessively ready when she arrived.

At ten past, my phone rang. Not glancing at the call display, I grabbed it at once, somehow sure that Maria was going to tell me I needed to find my own way to the club. Instead it was Caine.

"Anne, you sexy thing. What are you wearing?" she asked in a mischievous tone as my stomach turned little flip-flops of joy.

"Hi, handsome!" I said, striving for cool. "Never mind what I'm wearing, you dog. And what are you doing at this hour? It's one in the morning there."

"But seriously, are you dressed?" said Caine, muffling a snicker.

"Yeah, I'm dressed, boots and all. I'm waiting for Maria, who is, by the way, late. I should let you go. She'll be here any minute."

"No, I think you should talk to me," said Caine, and paused as a knock sounded. "Would that be someone at your door?"

Ready to chew playfully on Maria for her lateness, I crossed the short hallway and opened the door. It was not Maria. It was a very, very cute butch dyke. Reading from north to south, she had a short, sharp haircut, a shy smile, tight white tee, thick black leather belt, low-slung jeans, and brightly polished boots. I was instantly suspicious. What was an endangered species doing showing up in my townhouse complex?

"Can I help you?" I asked, meaning *Um, what?*

"Don't just stand there, let her in." Caine chuckled in my ear. "She's mine."

"Good evening, Ma'am," said the butch vision. "My name is Sammy. But you can call me anything you like."

Oh, it was like that, was it? "I've only got a minute," I said, regretfully. "I promised to—"

"Oh, Maria is in on it," said Caine, mirth rich in her tone. "She's standing you up tonight."

"Well, then, come in," I said to Sammy, who picked up a small suitcase that had been sitting out of sight by the doorjamb and squeezed past me in a respectful side shuffle. She headed immediately down the hall and turned into my office. Okay. She'd obviously been briefed.

"What's up, devious lover of mine?" I said to Caine.

"Oh, just let her do her thing," she said, still much too full of herself. "I miss you, and haven't seen you in months, and won't see you for another two months, and I just thought it's time you have a nice surprise."

"Was that a boot-polishing kit in that case?" I asked, heading down the hall to see what this cute stranger was doing in my office.

"Wait and see, my impatient one." said Caine.

In the office, Sammy had shut down my somewhat anti-quated computer. On the printer table, she had opened the brief-case, which held a very shiny laptop with an enormous screen, just booting up as I watched. Sammy dropped to her knees in an admittedly graceful movement and crawled under my desk, where she rooted around in the dust bunnies behind my CPU and emerged victorious with the high-speed network cable.

"You don't seem to have a wireless router," she explained briefly, at my inquiring glance.

She plugged the cable into the laptop and pulled a few other items from inside the case. I admired her deft touch with the computer almost as much as I'd admired her tight little ass when it had been sticking out from under my desk.

I gasped in delight as Caine appeared onscreen, holding a phone to her ear, her dark curls pulled back in a low pony-tail, resplendently butch in tight black shirt with no sleeves and leather chest harness. She was leaning back in her familiar over-stuffed desk chair.

"Can you see me?" she asked in my ear. "My indicator light is on."

"You've got a webcam!" I exclaimed.

"Ma'am, with your permission?" Sammy held up a small camera wrapped in loops of cord.

"Oh my, yes!" I laughed with sheer delight.

"I'm glad you like my idea," said Caine.

"Ma'am, one moment and I'll have sound," said Sammy. Another moment of fiddling and two tiny speakers made a chiming noise as she pulled up a dialog box on the screen and set up a skinny microphone on a spidery-looking stand.

"'Sir? If you want to try talking now?" said Sammy to Caine.

"'Scuse, darlin', while I switch gadgets." She put a headset on, pulled the mic in front of her admirably full lips. "How's this?" The sound of Caine's voice came clearly from the speakers.

"We're live at this end, Sir, Ma'am. The camera is sending."

"Wow, we're in living color!" I said with a feeling of awe as I closed my phone and dropped it in the pocket of my kilt.

"All for you to play with," said Caine in an ominously sexy tone, one hand resting casually on her leather-clad crotch. "And I do mean all of it. Boy, present!"

"Sir! Yes Sir!" Sammy dropped to her knees again in that oddly graceful gesture. She gazed at the floor and clasped her hands behind her back. "I'm here for your use and pleasure, if Ma'am should wish."

I looked at the screen, and then belatedly into the camera. "For me? What a thoughtful gift to help keep me warm tonight."

I took Sammy's chin in my hand, pulled her to face me. "You want to play with me? With us?"

"Yes Ma'am," said Sammy. "I surely would."

"Limits?" I asked

"Uh...Ma'am, I would prefer that my skin remain unbroken. And I have claustrophobia, so I can't do masks or hoods. And I don't do anything that involves animals, former food, former people, or heterosexual cisgendered men. Apart from that, I'm pretty open."

"Excellent!" I said, glancing at the screenful of Caine. "What a pretty boy you've sent me. I think I'd like to see more of her. Strip, Sammy."

Without demur, but with a show of slightly pink ears, Sammy peeled her shirt and then her sports bra over her head, revealing firm, medium-sized breasts with erect, very pink nipples. I was charmed already. She slowly unbuckled her leather belt, pulled it entirely free of her belt loops, and set it aside, a bit of attention to detail I admired. She then bent and unlaced her boots. Black leather, steel-toed, they looked both lived in and well cared for, with a shine that spoke of loving attention.

Sammy popped the buttons on her fly and peeled her jeans down her hips, her pale skin glowing in the strong light.

"Well, well, what have we here? What do you suppose that's for?"

"Um, Ma'am, I thought you might want...um...that is, to have use of me." Sammy was packing a moderately sized, realistic-looking hard dick, pushed low between her legs and protruding from a slackened nylon-strapped harness.

"Did you even warn her?" I asked Caine.

"No," said Caine, "I thought she'd find out about you soon enough."

"Ma'am, did I displease you in some way?"

"No, my cute boy, you did just fine. Leave your dick on, but tighten the harness."

As I spoke, I briskly unsnapped my kilt and unwound it from my hips, letting it drop.

Caine made an unmistakable chortling sound and Sammy's jaw dropped. I was sporting a dick myself, tucked through a soft, flexible leather harness and pulled down and strapped to my thigh. The strap was necessary to prevent causing a serious tilt to my kilt, because the silicone dick, while only medium-long, was tremendously thick.

"I thought you were going dancing!" said Caine.

"Yeah, I was going dancing! You never know who you're going to meet! It's freshly boiled and everything. Boy, go over to the top drawer in the dresser and fetch me the paddle and the red bag. I'm in a mood this evening, let's not waste time." I pulled a chair over to a position in front of the camera, stripped my

shirt off over my head, and sat down. "Good for you, honey?"
I asked Caine.

"Yeah, I can see perfectly."

Sammy came back and stood before me, shyly, holding my
lightweight carved wooden paddle and my drawstring bag of
tricks.

"Drop the bag, hand me that, and get over my lap, boy,"
I said, grinning, and she handed me the paddle and draped
herself obediently, with some awkwardness as she tried to figure
out where to place her dick so it was neither painful nor offen-
sive. She settled on letting it dangle between my thighs, and
made a soft startled sound when I grasped it with my knees. Her
pale, rounded butt cheeks flexed nervously, and I yanked at her
harness until the straps were spread as wide as possible, cupping
her cheeks firmly and leaving me lots of area to play with.

"I am really gonna enjoy this!" I said, and gave Sammy the
first ringing smack on her ass. She jumped a little and made a
choked sound low in her throat.

For fun, I chose to make the paddling a bit of an interrogation.

"Why'd you agree to do this?" Smack.

"Caine asked me t—" Smack.

"Do you do everything that Caine asks?"

"I try to do everyth—" Smack.

"What did you expect when you came in the door?"

"I'd seen pics of you, Ma'am, but—" Smack.

"How do you feel about being spanked while Caine watches?"

"It's kind of exciting and kind of embar—" Smack. Smack.
SMACK.

"Do you like a hard spanking, boy?"

"Oh God, I—" Smack.

Caine rubbed her hand meditatively over the leather crotch

of her pants, kneading slowly as she watched our scene.

"Oh yeah, look at her face when you hit her. She's trying to stay controlled."

"Then she's not doing very well," I said. "There's all these little gasping sounds, and she wriggles a lot after each whack. If I didn't have her cock between my knees, she might slide off my lap. And you know what else? Her cunt's getting juicy. I can see from here. She smells good, too."

Sammy whimpered with embarrassment, and I fancied I could see her ears getting pinker still. I decided to drop the interrogation and just concentrate on spanking, so I set about a slow, steady paddling that had her groaning and trembling by the time I stopped.

"Is that good, boy?" said Caine, watching intently.

"Sir, I...thank you. Thank you, Sir, Ma'am."

Her butt was swollen and uniformly red. Sammy hissed when I drew fingernails lightly across the scorching surface. I opened my knees and shoved her onto the floor legs-first. She landed gracefully, and I reached out and lifted her chin, directing her silently until she knelt in front of me as I sat in my chair.

After a moment's smiling contemplation of her flushed face and breasts, I opened my bag and pulled out nipple clamps and a length of cord. The clamps went on Sammy's nipples, with a bit of frantic air sipping from the poor boy, and the cord was easily looped around the chain between the clamps. I let the contraption drop and hang from her tits, saving it for later. I unfastened my cock from my thigh, and fed it, fat and hard, into her eager lips. The low sound of Caine's growl came from the small speakers.

From the insistent tugging and pushing on my cock, Sammy knew what she was doing, so I allowed her to set the rhythm of cocksucking. Watching Caine watch me get sucked off was good enough for a while, but soon it wasn't feeling aggressive enough for me, and I pulled my cock, trailing strings of drool, from Sammy's mouth, stood, and backed her up against the side of the desk. Crouched low on her knees, her head at the level of the desk edge, she was just the right height. I pulled up my cock and went in again, face-fucking the boy, who now had nowhere to go. Sammy's hands on my thighs pushed a little desperately at times, but she tried hard to keep up.

Caine couldn't see Sammy so well from this position, so I filled in the details for her, telling her how well Sammy sucked my cock and how bravely she was trying to please me. I described how she couldn't help herself and gagged every so often, and that her eyes were shiny with tears. I told Caine what a beautiful, beautiful boy Sammy was.

"I remember Sammy's cocksucking skills well," said Caine. "Last time she and I met up, I came in that very same hot mouth quite a few times."

"Oh, I'm not coming yet," I said, pulling out. Sammy wiped her wet mouth with the back of her hand, breathing hard and saying nothing. I grabbed a pile of books and CD folders from my desk and placed them on the floor as I spoke. "Bend over the end of the desk, no, the one opposite the laptop. Yeah, that's right, I want you looking right into the camera. Thighs up against the desk edge. Brace your arms. Spread your legs. Yeah, like that. Don't move."

Humming thoughtfully, I buckled Sammy's belt tightly around her naked waist. Then I pulled the cord attached to the nipple clamps forward across the desk and past the camera and fastened it to the base of my lamp with another cord from the red bag. I adjusted the laptop and camera to the new angle as Caine smiled at me, and I accidentally bumped the cord with the case, tugging Sammy's nipples. She grimaced.

"Tender tits, Sammy?"

"Yes Ma'am," she said hoarsely.

"You'd best try not to move too much, then."

I stopped to have a good look at what we were doing here. Caine was magnificent, even on the small screen: Her dark handsome face was a little flushed and the muscles in her arm flexed as she caressed her cunt through the leather. Sammy, sniffling slightly from the aftereffects of her enforced cocksucking, was bent over at the waist, braced on the desk, her tits pulled tight forward by clamps, her dick hanging forlornly under cherry-red ass cheeks.

I reached into my bag, snapped on a pair of nitrile gloves, and grabbed the lube. Before I opened the bottle, I reached around Sammy, slid a finger under her harness, past her hard clit, plunging into thick wet heat. Sammy groaned feelingly. "Ma'am, I...uh, oh damn."

"Mmm, she's wet," I said to Caine.

"Gonna fuck that boy?" said Caine, unfastening her pants and sliding her square-palmed, blunt-nailed hand within.

"Oh yeah. I'm gonna fuck this boy right now."

I squirted great gobs of lube into the palm of my gloved hand, pumped my cock once or twice, and slid inside her cunt a little too fast, trusting the vast amount of lube to smooth my way. Sammy's gasp sounded like an inward shriek, but I didn't wait for her to get used to the stout cock inside her and started a nice steady fuck, using her belt to pull her back against me with each thrust. Her paddled ass felt scorching hot against my thighs as I slid back and forth inside her, and the nipple clamps jingled merrily as her tits bounced.

"Describe for Caine what you're feeling."

"Yes Ma'am, uh, Sir, Ma'am's cock feels so big and so good inside my cunt, Sir, but my tits are jerking against the clamps each time she fucks me, and my ass hurts too, Sir."

Caine's hand, which had been moving slowly, sped up a little. I watched my lover jerk off. I watched my fat dick slide in and out of this hot sweet boy my lover had sent me, and through it all I was trying to hold back from coming. My clit twitched and throbbed, and I had to slow my rhythm so the feeling of the base of my dick shoving back at me didn't push me over the edge.

"Did you say your ass hurts?" I said, trailing my lubey finger down Sammy's ass crack.

"Um, my cheeks, Ma'am, my ass cheeks hurt where you spanked me," said Sammy in a panicked tone.

"You give me ideas, boy," I said happily, slowing my strokes still more. I squirted more lube into my palm, pulled back a little, and slowly pushed my thumb into Sammy's asshole.

"Oh, Ma'am," she said, feelingly.

"That sounds like a welcome." I pulled my dick, glistening, out of the boy's cunt, and as she gasped in surprise and loss, slid my lube-wet hand in a few fast pumps over the dick and nudged the head up against the boy's butthole.

"Oh Ma'am, oh, I don't know if I can...I've never had anything so thick up my ass. I just don't know—"

"Try, boy," growled Caine. "I'm pretty damn sure you can take it if you put your mind to it."

"I'll try, Sir, Ma'am. Oh! Oh!" This as the rounded head of my cock nosed its way inside her sphincter, as I leaned into Sammy, impatient with the necessity for care.

"C'mon, boy, let me in!" And I spanked her fiery ass a few more times as she made a high-pitched gasping noise; my clit was hard and cunt clenching from the sensation of my dick pressing against my clit, and then her asshole suddenly loosened and the bulbous head slipped inside with a rush. Her ass clamped tight around the smooth shaft, and I paused with only an inch or two inside, letting her adjust. She hung her head and made little panicky noises. I leaned over Sammy and grabbed the hair atop her head, just long enough for my fingers to find purchase, and pulled her head up to face the camera.

"She broke into a fine sweat, with just the tip inside," I informed Caine, who was breathing heavily. "I'm not even all the way in. Wanna see what happens next?"

"God, that's hot," said Caine. "Yeah, show me what you do with this boy of mine."

"Sammy, how about you?"

"Ma'am, Sir, I'm up for going anywhere you both want to take me." Still a bit panicky, Sammy's voice was nevertheless earnest, and I was touched to my perverted core by her trust and willingness. It made me want to take her as high as she could go.

With my hand still fisted in her brush cut so she was panting open-mouthed into the camera's greedy eye, I gave in to my burning desire to get all the way inside this boy. Trembling from desire and feeling myself right at the edge of a hot wet orgasm, I fed the entire length of my cock into her ass, going slow so she almost had a chance to get used to the stretch before another inch slipped inside and she gasped anew. I stopped when my hips flattened her sore red ass cheeks. Sammy's gasps sounded almost like a wheeze now, and I held completely still, fighting my too-close orgasm.

Caine knew the look. "Maybe you should just go ahead and come," she said slyly. "I'm right there with you. Plus, if you're interested in allowing it, Sammy can come almost instantly if she puts her mind and hand to it."

"God, I...I don't think I can wait anymore; you are both too fucking hot. Boy, if you can come while I do, you've got permission. Otherwise, let's finish this ride." And I let go the control and let go the hesitation and let go of being the careful top.

I gladly accepted the beautiful submission offered by Sammy, and I abandoned my grip on her hair and grabbed her hips, and I fucked her ass hard and fat and long and fast, really digging in on the instroke so the pressure from the base of my cock hit that perfect spot over my clit. Sammy squealed at the first hard thrust, then shoved both hands underneath herself, falling forward onto her clamped nipples in a way that had to hurt in a way both delightful and awful. I knew by the flex of her arms that she was jerking off, although I couldn't tell if she was holding her dick or frantically rubbing her clit behind the harness, and absentmindedly decided to ask her later because right now I...just...didn't care.

Caine sat there on the computer screen, her eyes burning, fixed on me and Sammy, one hand holding her pants away from her cunt, the other hand a blur over her clit. And amazingly, though I'd been so fucking close to coming for so long, it was Caine who came first, hips bucking upward, full lips snarling beautiful filth, and then Sammy cried out, her tone suddenly more pleasure than pain. Her ass had been stretched so tight around my thick shaft that I could actually feel her asshole pulse as she started her come, and that tipped me over and everything vanished in a hot blind roar of sensation and our three voices in a harmony of squeals and growls and my hips pumping, pumping until vision returned and I panted to a halt with my knees weak and my clit thrumming.

Before I slid my dick out of Sammy's ass, I leaned over her lovely sweat-coated back, fished her breasts to the side as she groaned in foreknowledge, and took off both nipple clamps at precisely the same instant. The pain of the outraged nerves firing back to life took Sammy's breath away, and her body silently shuddered taut against me, grinding against my oversensitive clit. From that and her pain I came again, a small one this time, thrusting tiny little gentle strokes until the last little bubbles of come had popped in my cunt and heart and mind and dick, and all I felt was a truly massive benevolence toward both these sweet butches.

"Thank you, gentlemen." I carefully pulled my dick out of Sammy's tender ass as she squeaked softly, unbuckled my harness one-handed, looked around, and deftly dropped the whole thing into my wastepaper basket for later cleanup. Sammy, still slumped over my desk, peeked at me over her shoulder, obviously in a welter of shyness. Weak-kneed, I tottered over to my desk chair and collapsed into it with a grateful groan.

Caine laughed delightedly from the computer screen. "I'm going to log off now, love. You and Sammy look like you need some recovery time. Call you both tomorrow?"

I readily acquiesced. Sammy blushingly wriggled her fingers in a parting wave at the camera, and I clicked the End button. Caine's knowing grin winked out of existence like the Cheshire cat, and I turned to regard Sammy, who had sunk exhaustedly to her knees. She gave me a dizzying smile.

Aftercare was going to be a real pleasure.

SPOILED

Shawna Elizabeth

She spoiled me. When I walked in the door I was so happy to see her I barely noticed she had a whole pile of presents waiting for me, all laid out on the floor. I was gone for weeks, visiting my family for the holidays. Being away made me appreciate how much better I feel in the city where I live now. My girlfriend's house felt more like my home.

She told me to open the gifts and then stood back to watch. I settled down in the middle of the room and started tearing through the ribbons and tissue paper. I uncovered my favorite perfume, lacy panties, and a tiny box containing a delicate strand of pearls. "Because you are classic," she said.

"It's too much!" I exclaimed. I was cradling the gifts in my arms, surrounded by torn paper. She grinned sheepishly, full of pride.

"Come on," she said, reaching for my arm and pulling me up off the floor. I embraced her and she held me for a moment. Then she pushed me and my head connected with the wall, my hair splayed out behind me. She was full of surprises. Her hands caught my shoulders, pinning me and holding my body taut. She moved her arms down the length of my body, getting reacquainted with my curves.

She pushed my dress up and I thrust out my thigh so she could see the stockings I had worn the whole plane ride back, just for her. She grabbed a fistful of the flesh above the tight band of my stocking and I started working my knee between her legs, rubbing against the thick fabric of her pants. She stood a little below me—I was taller than her in my heels—but she was forceful; she had me trapped against the wall, still reeling from the moment I had made impact. She loosened her grip and I faltered a little as I tried to walk away.

She was utterly composed as she led me up the narrow staircase and down the hall. The light was dim in her attic bedroom on the top floor of the house. She took me in her arms and kissed me beneath the slanted ceiling, everything in her room comfortable and close. She turned on some music and I went to sit on the bed, wondering if I should take my high heels off or leave them on. I waited for her. She usually told me what to do.

"Hi baby," she said when she walked over to the bed. She was looking at me, drinking me in; there was such appreciation in her eyes. I spread my knees and she leaned down to kiss me, standing between my legs at the edge of the bed. She cupped my face, caressed my neck, and smoothed my hair.

Then she eased my body back until I was lying on the bed. She moved my legs further apart. I felt shy but she said, "It's okay, I just want to look at you." She pulled my dress to my hips and reached up to give my tits one hard squeeze over my clothes. Then she knelt between my legs. She ran her hands across the slippery silk of my stockings. She pressed the flat of her palm against my pubic mound, pressing in and then hooking one finger beneath the waistband of my panties, sliding them along my skin.

The panties were a fancy pair she'd never seen before, covered in scalloped French lace. But she wasn't admiring the panties; she was pulling them off, down past my knees, easing them over my shiny heels. Then she spread my thighs and looked right at my naked flesh, my little pink pussy completely shaved and soft. I felt hot between my legs just knowing she was looking at me. She leaned forward and spread my lips, staring longer than I felt comfortable with.

"God, your pussy is fucking beautiful," she said, putting me at ease. I felt her hot breath and the downy fuzz on her chin. The first brush of her lips made me shiver. She started tracing my folds with her tongue, refamiliarizing herself with their topography.

I let out a girlish moan; it had been weeks since I felt such an intimate touch, and the pleasure was exquisite. Her tongue dipped slightly into my opening, gently feeling out its borders. She pressed one finger inside me as her tongue moved to my clit and began to work more intentionally. I extended my arms out along the bed and grabbed fistfuls of the covers, pressing her head with my thighs, my eyes squeezed shut. I felt the rush of orgasm seep through me, making me melt down into the bed. I tried to look at her, waiting for her head to pop up, but she just kept licking and pleasuring me. I came again almost at once, this time in a short burst. A bead of sweat trailed down my inner thigh. She did not move, she held her position, dutifully attending to my pussy. I came a third time, my legs quaking. She held my ankles and pressed my feet down on the floor. I dug my fingers into my own hair and scratched at my scalp, experiencing two more climaxes in rapid succession, completely crazy from coming so hard and so fast.

She stood up and we both lay down on the bed, holding one another. Even after giving me so much pleasure, she looked at me with gratitude. "You just made me come five times!" I said, still reeling.

"Well, I needed to show you how much I missed you. You know, to make up for lost time." I giggled and nuzzled my face into hers. My hands explored the broadness of her chest and squeezed the wide expanses of her arms. She undressed me and took off most of her clothes. She lay on top of me and I buried my whole face in her tits. She kissed my neck and I ran my hands down her back, letting my nails trail down her sides. I liked the weight of her on top of me; I felt blissed out and full of love.

Then I looked up and saw a change in her eye, some darkness clouding over the sparkling green. "Were you a good girl when you were gone, baby?" I instantly felt small and nervous; I couldn't find my voice.

I thought back to the time I had spent away from her in my hometown. I missed her, I stayed in touch, but I wasn't exactly beyond reproach. A few days in my father's house and I was itching to get out. I couldn't stand the closed in feeling and the conversations I overheard through the walls. I felt myself slipping into old patterns reminiscent of teen angst and rebellion. I needed to be around other queers. I caught the train down to the city and found my high school friends. Pretty soon we were gathered around a mirror primping, gossiping, and drinking wine. Then we all headed out together to a dance party.

I really had the best intentions, but it's hard not to attract attention at party when you're full of anxious energy and all dressed up. Call it the curse of the lonely femme. My friends were on the dance floor, and I was sitting at the bar by myself. Most of the dykes in the room were androgynous hipster types with choppy haircuts, clad head to toe in haphazard thrift-store finds. Not really my style. I was so caught up watching my friends across the dance floor and nursing my drink that I didn't notice the only cute butch in the place had sidled up next to me.

"Hey, you look bored," she said. "Are you from out of town?" She was leaning right into me, shoving her hands in the back pockets of her jeans. Her moves were bold, her half smile full of swagger. I let her refill my drink. It burned in my throat and my cheeks flushed red as she stared at me. She was practically licking her lips.

Pretty soon my friends were over the party and told me they wanted to leave. I leaned over to the butch and spoke directly into her ear: "Hey, I gotta go."

"Let me walk you to the streetcar." She held the door for me and we walked across the street to the stop. She put her arms on my shoulders and pressed me firmly against the safety glass of the shelter. I was caught off guard and still warmed up from the free drink and flirtation. She bent down to kiss me, and her breath tasted like whiskey. My girlfriend doesn't drink. Actually, this butch was nothing like my girlfriend; she was kind of tall, lanky, and old school. The strangeness of this new girl on the street was turning me on, kissing her seemed seedy and indecorous. She started feeling me up and squeezing my tits through my clothes. In that instant, the streetcar clambered up.

I managed to find my voice, but only a tiny sound emanated from inside me. "I missed you so much, Daddy. I promise I was good."

"Daddy missed you, too, baby girl," she snarled. "But I also know what a brat you can be, how much attention you need. We have to get you back in line." It was like she could read my surreptitious thoughts and see my indiscretion. I tried to banish the remembrance of that anonymous stolen kiss on the street.

She flipped me over onto my stomach and spread my legs wide. She started kissing my back, which tickled and made me squirm.

"Hold still," she commanded. She peeled my stockings off one at a time and used them to tie my hands to the metal railing of the headboard.

Then she kissed the cheeks of my ass. She grabbed a handful of each cheek and squeezed it hard, then lightly ran her hand over it again. The flesh was jumping under her touch, feeling fine-tuned and electric. She brought her hand down with a stinging slap. She kept slapping one side of my ass until it burned, and then she moved down to my inner thigh.

"This ass is mine," she said. She leaned down and licked my pussy between my legs from the back; it was still so sensitive from before that I gasped. "You think just anybody can give you what you need?" She slapped me again, harder and harder, and I started to cry out. I wanted to be good for her, to take everything she gave, but I couldn't hold it in, I shrieked from the sting of it. "You need it, little brat, you need me to keep you in line, and I know you have been missing this. You little slut."

"I'm only *your* slut," I screamed. I didn't want her to stop, but my legs were twitching and flinching away from the blows, so she let up.

She untied my wrists. They were covered in red marks; my hands pulsed as the blood rushed back. My fine stockings were stretched out and ruined; she tossed them crumpled on the floor. She flipped me over and then walked away from the bed. I was shivering and naked, my face twisted to the side. When she came back she was tightening the leather straps of her harness around her thick thighs. She kissed my face and I relaxed. Her lips were comforting; I brushed her shaggy hair to the side and cradled her head.

"I'm going to fuck you," she said, and I actually heard myself whimper with longing, "but first you're gonna suck Daddy's dick."

She straddled me and eased her cock between my lips; I was straining to take her into me, the fleshy silicone hardness of her cock in my mouth. My mouth was watering and I used the wetness to take in more of her, grasping the base and guiding more length inside. "Oh, that's a good girl, suck on Daddy's dick." The cries caught in my throat as she pushed in harder and harder. She was so deep in the back of my throat I was gagging and short of breath; she pulled my hair and kept thrusting in and out, fucking my face and using me. "Look how you love that cock, you fucking little slut." Suddenly she pulled out and slapped her dick against my face, flinging my own hot spit across my cheek. My eyes sutured shut, my eyebrows clamped together, my face was covered in spit and seeping tears. She felt my pussy and it was soaking wet. She held her dripping cock in her fist and pressed it into me. It felt huge.

I hadn't been fucked in so long I didn't know if I could take it. "It's too much!" I gasped.

"Relax," she said "You're a good girl, you can take it, take all of this dick. It's big and hard because of you." I started rocking my hips to meet her and felt more of her length and strength. She kissed me and then pushed down on my neck so firmly I couldn't breathe.

When she let go, I caught my breath and wailed, "I want you to touch me." I loved getting fucked with the dick, but I needed the friction of her inside me. I needed to feel her hand bearing down and bringing the maximum contact that I could stand. She pulled out and reached over to grab some lube. My pussy was dripping wet, swollen, and throbbing. She spread me and slapped my pussy with her left hand. She flicked my clit with her thumb and forefinger, and it stung. I was grateful for the torment; my guilt was subsiding. She covered her right hand with the lube. It felt cold and slick when she eased it into me, and the coldness provided relief. She started pressing and twisting into me as I writhed on the sheets. My hips ground down. I could feel her fingers against the delicate barrier of my ass from the inside. I tried to keep my breath steady and regular. "Oh, it feels good," I gasped.

"Your pussy's good, baby," she said and pressed in harder with all of her power. I could feel her flex and coil her hand, like she was grasping me from the inside, and filling me up. "You take it so well." I started getting delirious; the preternatural noises I was making sounded hollow in my ears and far away. My nipples were hard, my tits beaded with sweat. Her whole fist was inside me, I knew it, but it seemed like something else, something more, like all of her was pounding me from the inside, obliterating me. I had been punished and now I was pure again. I started screaming, "Oh my God," and felt a rush and surge as my pussy gushed liquid onto the bed. She pulled out and I shook and gasped for air. Her face lost its dark intensity and softened with pride.

"Thank you, I love you, I missed you so much," I sputtered. I clung to her and rolled myself up, curling into her, pressing our bodies together. She kissed my forehead and squeezed me tight in her strong arms.

"Next time, don't leave me, baby girl."

I knew I wouldn't leave her. She'd spoiled me for anybody else.

GENTLEMAN CALLER

Sossity Chiricuzio

You've got a job interview today and have traded in your skinny jeans for well-pressed slacks, with all the accompanying bits in place: button-down shirt, tie, and narrow belt—the subtle wingtip details on your shoes the only obvious nod to your fag sensibilities. I'm looking at you, all proper and focused, and I can't stop thinking about how I want to sit on your lap and muss your hair while murmuring dirty suggestions into the sensitive hollow of your ear. It feels so odd to be drawn by this business drag, until I realize it's because your gender makes it queer; your brain, perverse. You catch me out, eyeing you, and I refuse to answer your unspoken question until you promise to wear it for me later. Eyes narrowed, you nod, and I say that you look like someone who can afford some...expensive...company. Your grip on my arm, and the quirk of my grin, are all the negotiation we need.

Evening has finally come, after hours of forced productivity and delightful anticipation, and I'm waiting in your room for you to come home. Our love of the game makes the simple gesture of your knock on the door the key to a different reality—one where you are indeed that businessman with a pocket full of cash and pent-up lust, ending a hard day's work with a stop at your favorite house of ill repute. There's a rumor of a new girl, and breaking them in is your especial pleasure. We stand on either side of one inch of wood and feel the energy building, crackling, until I almost expect a spark from the doorknob when I finally let you in.

I set the stage with a pink nightie so pale it's just this side of virginal white, and so thin it's more naked than skin, flowing over my creamyfat curves. My hair is down, and so is my gaze—it's apparent this is the first time I've ever entertained a client and that I'm both anxious to please and reluctant to start. A perfect mix for your cruel gentleman's tastes, and you're obviously controlling yourself as you take in my appearance. There are only two places to sit in the room—the bed, and an easy chair. I opt for the chair as less of a commitment and try to lead you to it, only to be brought up short by your hand at the back of my head, swinging me around and forcing me to look up.

You look deep, searching for my weak spots, and a sign of my desire, and I feel myself slip fully into character—softening for you, scared, but only of getting what I want, or disappointing you. Riding the edge of eager and terrified. Your hand moves up, into my hair, grabbing a fistful and tugging, gently, down, until kneeling is the only option.

"Do you know what to do?" you ask, and my nod is not acceptable—another tug, harder, and I say, "Yes, sir," and slowly reach for your belt buckle. It's a simple mechanism, but feeling your eyes on me makes me clumsy, and it seems to take forever to get it unclasped.

Your cock is obvious under the fine weave of your slacks,

and I pause for a second, almost overwhelmed by the thoughts of what is to follow, until you tug my hair again and threaten to ask for another girl. I quickly reach to unbutton and unzip, and then hesitate again—unsure if I should pull your briefs down or reach through the fly.

You growl and pull your cock out, holding me in place while you brush the head of it against my lips. "You're gonna use that pretty mouth on me now, and make it good." I can only nod as you're already pushing in, barely gentle.

There's no time to think, or plan, and no way to resist. I become a series of reactions as you fuck my mouth: inhaling whenever I'm able, swallowing you down, using my tongue in every way that might increase your pleasure as you move over every surface of my mouth. Your breath comes harsher, and the grip in my hair tightens until I'm sure you'll come, and I brace myself. The shock of you pulling away leaves me open-mouthed and blinking, and you chuckle, low and harsh.

"Get on the bed." I scramble to obey. You remove your shoes and slacks and kneel over me, looking at me until I long to close my eyes, but I don't quite dare.

"You are mine for the night, and that means I get to do whatever I want to you. Right?" I nod, and again, it's not enough. You slap my face, obviously more lightly than you'd like, and tell me to "Use your words, girl."

"Yes, sir," I manage to say before you slide your hand under my nightie, making me startle, and I start to pull away until the look in your eyes makes me freeze. Your fingers brush over my clit and plunge inside, briefly, and your smirk at my wetness makes my breath catch.

"You can say no if you want to, but I don't believe you, and I won't stop," you say before sliding your fingers into my mouth. The taste of myself, and the inevitability of what is to come, melts away the last of my resistance, and you see it and know you've won. It is this knowledge of my deepest places, in body and mind, that makes your dominance so compelling, and the orchestra of your own deviance that makes it so richly satisfying.

"I'm not done with your mouth, not at all. Open up for me and spread your legs, and take what I give you." You slide your cock in, past my lips and further down my throat from this angle, and watch me work to breathe around it. All I can see is your face, far above, cruel and hungry and relentless. You fist one hand in my hair and reach back with the other, between my legs, and begin to fuck me, moving with, and against, the rhythm you set with your hips. I moan and you tell me that I better not stop sucking your cock, or come, until you say so. I'm every kind of vulnerable, and so far into submission there's no question of disobeying.

I can feel my orgasm building, deeper and higher, and I'm crying with the effort of holding it back, and you sense it and stop, pulling out of me so suddenly and leaving me so achingly open that I almost hate you for it. It shows in my expression, and you simply watch, full of brute enjoyment and power.

"What do you want?" you ask, and I, momentarily rebellious, refuse to answer. The slap you give me leaves no doubt how gentle you were being before, and you make it clear you're not going to ask again.

"You want me to fuck you, we both know it. Truth is, I'm going to do it anyway. The only question is if I let you come when I do."

I want it, I do, and it's entirely possible you'll follow up the threat, so I answer quickly this time. "I want you to fuck me..." and you're already shaking your head, it's not enough, and I try again. "I want you to fuck me, sir, please." You grin and move down, between my legs, and stroke your cock, and my clit, so slowly. I try again, with every bit of sweetness I can muster through the haze of need: "Please sir, please...I want you, I do...please." You toss your tie over your shoulder and push into me hard and fast, and again, pounding into me until the whole bed moves.

"That's right, sweet whore, give it to me..." And I am, arms and legs wrapped tight around you, sobbing and moaning and begging without words, right where I want to be. "Mine, all mine," you whisper in my ear, and I am, in this endless moment, all yours. "Come for me, now!" and I do, crying out in a voice hoarse from trying to form your name, shaking and shuddering underneath you. Again and again, I come when you tell me, until my tears, and our sweat, have thoroughly soaked your dress shirt and I can hardly move.

You shift onto your side and pull me into you, stroking my hair and kissing me, soft and lingering. The deep tide of cruel-edged passion turned to tenderness and our wells filled up, sated and sinking into each other, we sleep. Your quiet voice, before dream takes me: "That's my good girl..." And I am: your good, sweet girl, your dirty whore, your love.

THREE WEEKS AND TWO DAYS

Meridith Guy

'm bent over the sawhorse I made, panting. My legs are spread wide. We're in the narrow space between a beating and fucking and she's giving me a moment to rest. I lean hard on my elbows to relieve some of the pressure in my legs, and I can feel her watching me from behind as I rise up on my tiptoes and back down, stretching both my calves and the ache running through my thighs and stomach. I wonder what exactly she's looking at. The marks she put on my skin? The sweat on my back? My thigh muscles trembling? She's about to fuck me and it's going to hurt. I can't wait.

As of this morning it had been three weeks and two days since she last fucked me. I'd given up teasing her. Stopped planting myself in front of her when she rounded a corner. Stopped snaking a hand over the skin of her thighs at night. I'd almost even given up longing, though that ache was proving harder to shake. In frustration, I had begun trying to practice Buddhist non-attachment. It was a mantra: *I don't care if she fucks me (or not). I don't care if she beats me (or not).* It wasn't working.

Even though I was about to end up ass over ears on a sawhorse, nothing seemed different that morning over breakfast or, for that matter, during any of the other routine things we did that day. We bought corn and onions at the market. We stopped for iced coffee at the bistro on the corner. Later, she pulled on a white tank and jeans to mow the lawn and I watched her sweat in the sun from inside the cool house, feeling warmer than I should have in the air-conditioning. I might have been trying to practice indifference, but I was getting wet watching her arms flex as she forced the mower over the hilly yard, dirt and grass eddying around her. It had been three weeks and two days, and even from behind a pane of glass she was fanning the heat smoldering inside me.

This is where I was standing, eyes closed, swirling melting ice cubes in a glass and picturing her running her hands slowly down over my hips, when I felt her breath hot on my neck. Her voice was low when she spoke, and it hummed right over my clit. "Watching me? Do you like what you see?"

I shivered without meaning to. After all, I had heard her boots thumping across the floor. Knew she was coming up behind me. I didn't expect to feel the summer heat radiating off her skin or for her to smell so deliciously dusty and hot. Without opening my eyes, I said, "The lawn is lovely." And that's how I ended up over the sawhorse.

Before I even finished speaking, she pulled my arms hard behind me and wrenched my wrists together, clasping them in one hand. My drink dropped, scattering ice over the carpet, and she shoved me against the window, pressing my cheek to the glass. Looping her fingers in my hair, she yanked my head back hard and leaned over me, teeth too close to my throat. "I'm standing behind you like this and you're talking about the lawn? I might beat you right here."

For three weeks and two days I would have sworn that those words were all I wanted to hear. Now that she was saying them, her fingertips digging into my wrists, I'd have settled for a gentle fuck and some adoration. I whimpered as she pulled my head back further and pressed me harder against the window. With a chuckle, she reached around me and slid her fingers between my thighs. I blushed seconds before she slipped her fingers inside me, knowing I was already dripping.

Jerking my arms back and hauling me away from the glass, she shoved me toward the basement door. I stumbled in front of her, focusing on not falling down the stairs without my hands to balance me. I struggled to keep my bare feet from slipping under the soles of her boots, but by the sound of her laughter I could tell she wouldn't mind if my clumsiness got me a few extra bruises on the way to the sawhorse. By the time we got there, my cheeks were burning and she gave me a split second to shake out my arms before she grabbed my hip, pulled me back, and with her other hand, shoved me down over the sawhorse.

It wasn't the first time I'd been in this position. Having watched me build a pair of sawhorses in a fit of ambition, she patiently waited until it was clear (almost immediately) that I wasn't going to actually construct anything on them and then repurposed them for all-around play and punishment. Even more humiliating than being dripping wet on my own sawhorse was admitting I'd considered that possibility when I measured the wood to determine the height.

She held me down, pressing her hand solidly against my lower back as I tucked my elbows underneath me and tried to catch my breath. She kicked my ankles apart, spreading my legs and sending a chill sliding down my thighs. I was getting more and more wet. She left another cool spot on my back when she stepped back and moved her hand away, lightly brushing over my skin. Feeling panic tight in my throat, I mentally paged through the implements she might have brought to the basement. What floggers and paddles had she brought down? Were the canes here? Had she brought her dick? What about the one that was too big?

I was still flipping through images in my head, trying to relax my muscles even though my heart was pounding, when her hand cracked against my ass. I yelped and bucked closer to the sawhorse. With each successive smack she spoke to me, though I had to struggle through the biting pain to understand her.

"For three weeks and two days I have watched you hint around. I've had to listen to you whine about being touched. I want you to know that I'm going to touch you when and where I feel like and not because you're tugging at my sleeves." She was panting softly when she finished speaking, and she hit me twice more before she stopped. "Do you understand?"

I understood, but I couldn't tell her that. I couldn't tell anyone that, because I couldn't quite breathe. I gasped for air, skin burning from the middle of my ass to the tops of my thighs. She hadn't spanked me that hard in months, and that was for dropping an egg on the floor and asking her to clean it up. I was still thinking about what happened after the last beating when she raked her nails up over my bottom. "Well?" The sharp pain was excruciating and I choked out a yes. It wasn't fast enough.

I heard her step back and rustle briefly in a bag. I didn't have time to think about what was about to happen before she brought the paddle down hard on my ass. In seconds I was yelling that I understood, yes, yes, please stop. I sprinkled in a couple of curses, but it only resulted in her hitting me harder. My voice sounded ragged as I cried. I twisted slightly, trying to avoid the blinding pain from the blows she was raining down on my skin, rising onto my tiptoes and sinking down again. Knowing better than to move away but absolutely unable to be still.

I began to plead. "Please stop. Oh, please. I can't take it!" We went on like that for a while, she spanked and I pleaded, long enough to feel like my tender butt had swollen and had gotten so raw that even a breeze would feel like too much pressure. When she finally stopped, it took me a second to register the silence. It was then that she pinched me hard, one hand on my nipple, the other on the sensitive, red skin of my bottom. My voice was raspy when I screamed and I realized I must have been making more noise during the beating than I thought.

The part of me that could still think clearly realized that the pinch was lasting longer than usual, as she slowly loosened her grip and then squeezed again. I arched my back in agony, unable to move away as she alternately rolled my nipple between her thumb and forefinger and dug her nails into the searing skin on my ass. Switching, she gently massaged that spot on my bottom while she squeezed my nipple hard. Jerking away from pain and leaning into pleasure didn't work; she simply switched which hand was inflicting the torment. All of her fingers were on a direct line to my clit. Squirming, I tried to make myself relax a little into the throbbing, stinging ache. If I was thinking at all, it was to wonder, not for the first time, how I could like this so much.

But I did like it, very much, and I knew what would be coming next. I was going to get fucked for the first time in three weeks and two days. It was going to hurt. She was going to like it. And that would be before she even got around to penetrating my ass. I leaned over the sawhorse and waited.

COUNTING
LOVE

August InFlux

I am loved. I know this. Not the same way other people know this, of course. I don't get flowers. I don't get chocolates. I don't get little cards with Hallmark greetings on them. I don't want those things. In my book, stupidity defines traditional romance. It gives no thought to your partner's innate uniqueness. It's trite. And it doesn't get you laid nearly as well. You have to show your love in different ways with different people.

Remember how I showed you that I loved you the other day?

I texted you every hour. I could just picture you, bent over your desk, trying to focus on getting that press release done, this receipt forwarded to Finance, that e-mail sent to so-and-so. You were supposed to be concentrating. Don't you have things to do? Pictures of my new outfit, presented in pieces. Commentary in between. Pink Keds. Tennis socks. *I like tennis, don't you?* Little pink skirt. (I'm not such a huge fan of the color, but I know you like me in it. I wanted to show you that I think of you even when we're not together.) *Like my skirt, Daddy?*

White blouse, with the puffed cap sleeves. *The buttons pop off easy.* Young.

Fast-forward to your return home from work. I bounded off the couch to greet you, a silly smile dancing on my lips. Complete in my new outfit. You dropped your jacket and briefcase next to the door and took me gently into your arms. I fit so well there. The hug got tighter. The hand cupping the back of my head grabbed a fistful of hair and dragged my lips up to yours. Heat flooded my body.

"You," you whispered, quietly enunciating each word, "have been very bad today." I started to tremble.

Fast-forward.

You threw me on the bed, and I kept whispering, "No, no, no," but you kept coming at me. Telling me what a little cocktease I was. Saying you were going to teach me a lesson about teasing men. You grabbed my hair to force my head back to look at you. You had me scared in such a good way, leaning over me like that.

You said, "You've been a bad girl." No flourish. Just said it like you would to a little girl who'd done something wrong. "And now I'm going to take you like you deserve to be taken."

"Oh, Daddy, please no," I breathed. You tied my wrists together, then tied them to a length of cord attached to the headboard. Excitement ran like fire through my veins. "Daddy, please don't, I'll be so good."

You grabbed my head again and whispered viciously, "Now you listen to me: You do what I say when I say it, and maybe you'll get off on a light punishment. Clear?" You shook my head once for emphasis.

"Yes."

"Yes what?"

"Yes, Daddy."

"Good. Roll over."

"Yes, Daddy." I turned over onto my elbows, ass in the air, my little pink skirt falling over my cheeks. My shoes and socks sat neatly on the floor next to the bed, near where my blouse fell when you ripped it off.

You smoothed my skirt over my ass as you took off your belt.

"Count to five."

"Yes, Daddy." The thick leather thudded against my ass. "One." It wasn't that hard. I know you're just warming me up. Again. "Two." A few more strokes. I'm disappointed: they're too soft. Just swipes to get the blood flowing. I want more.

"Five." You rub my ass in consolation. But I'm greedy. "Daddy..."

Your hand tightens on my skin, fingers dig into the muscle. "Daddy, I..."

"Do you have something you need to tell me?"

I nod. My mouth opens and closes.

Nails scrape. "Were you bad?"

"Yes." *Slap.* "Yes, Daddy."

"What did you do?" Dangerously kind.

"I—"

Slow, pronounced, "Did you let someone touch you?"

Whispered, "Yes."

"What did you let them do?"

"I let them touch me—down there. Where you said only you should touch me."

Slap. "Bad girl. Did you enjoy it?"

"No—"

Slap. "I bet you did enjoy it, didn't you? You filthy little slut."

"Daddy, it just felt so good."

Slap. Harder this time. "And you couldn't help yourself, could you? You little whore. Whores get punished."

"No!"

"Yes." Your hand runs up under my skirt, shoving it up off my ass. "Ask for it." I hesitate. *Slap.*

"Say, 'please, Daddy, punish me.'" Fingers tease my slick wet lips and my mind blanks in ecstasy. I struggle to come back to the present.

"Please—punish me, please."

"So polite." *Smack.* Your hand against my ass. "But you forgot something."

"Please, Daddy, punish me."

"Good girl." *Smack.* "Count to ten."

The belt returns, this time with enough force to sting harshly upon impact without the fabric barrier. It leaves my skin humming pleasantly, vibrating. I gasp sharply with each stroke. Each thud hurts more than the last.

Thud. Gasp. "Eight."

Thud. Squeak. "Nine."

Thud. Whine. "Ten."

You set the belt down as your hands run over my burning ass cheeks. Your hands massage my body as you bend over to growl into my ear, "Those little noises you make turn me on so much."

"Yes, Daddy?"

"Yes." You flip me over harshly, suddenly. I inhale sharply, trying to untwist my arms to a slightly more comfortable position. "I'm going to put my cock inside you and pump until I come."

My legs draw up to my torso. You know I love it on my back. "No, Daddy," I plead. I watch as you stand and drop your jeans, roll a condom onto the hard length of your dick. Cyberskin's a bitch to clean. You crawl back onto the bed, knock my knees out of your way.

"Yes."

"Daddy, it won't fit," I protest. "Your cock's too big, Daddy. My pussy's too little."

"I like a tight pussy like yours, little girl." You say the last two words with such possession I nearly come right there.

"You want—you want to fuck my tight pussy, Daddy?"

"Yes." Your fingers are rubbing my cunt now, slicking up the entrance. You slide one in. Then two.

I moan, "Oh Daddy, please no," as my eyes roll back into my head. A twisted game we play, where no means yes.

Your fingers slide out abruptly, the next second they're entangled once again tightly in my hair. Your face an inch from mine, you snarl, "You are here for my pleasure, you little slut." With that, you grab both my ankles in one hand and pin them off to the side. In one swift motion you've shoved your cock inside me and have started pounding away at my cunt. "I will take my pleasure in you."

Little shrieks escape my lips. Pleasure and pain combine, and I grab the tie holding my hands for security. Your words help turn the pain into solid pressure, and I lose myself in them.

"Such a good girl, taking my cock like this. Such a tight little pussy. Such a good girl." One hand runs over my breasts, tweaking my nipples in passing.

"Oh, God, Daddy, you feel so good," I breathe. Your fingernails rake over my ass, and I scream silently as the burn from the beating flares up. My body begins to shudder uncontrollably, and you pound me faster. I can tell you're close by the way you're breathing. The harness must be hitting you just right. Every ridge of your dick hits my inside walls and I squeeze you. I know you can feel it. Hold you there for a millisecond. Your eyes roll back briefly and you look at me like I'm the most amazing thing in the world, and thrust deeper. My body shudders again and you flick a finger across my swollen clit. I shriek. The minute sensation sends me over the edge and I come with only the thought in my head of you taking your pleasure in me. Your movements in and out of my cunt prolong my orgasm and I open my eyes as I ride it out with you. Eyes locked, you don't give me a break as I come down. You start pounding harder. Faster. Having your way with me. Using me with only the thought of your own pleasure in mind. As you start to come, you yell out. Thumb my clit again and there I am right there with you. Falling. Through ecstasy. Screaming my release.

I remember to inhale after a minute or so. Our breathing slows, and I look at you, your face shining. You start to pull out, and I stop you.

"Please. Stay. Just for a bit." You nod. Our senses calm. The fan on the far side of the room blows cool air over our hot bodies. When I finally signal you to come out, you crawl up next to me. Release my wrist bindings. Curl up behind me. Kiss my neck, my face, my lips, my nose, my shoulder.

"Such a good girl," you whisper, one arm wrapping around me.

I kiss you. "Thank you, Daddy." I know that I am loved.

PURGE

Maria See

We are in your bedroom after the drive to your home from the airport. Like always, I wasted little time before crawling on top of you and my lips wasted little time before they too were on top of yours.

I reacquaint myself with your skin and your smell. I never know, each time I leave you, when or if I will see you, this way, again.

I roll a few inches away from you and lock my eyes to yours. There is something more I want to see. *I want to see you in your collar.*

"Will you get my bag? I left it near the front door."

You leave the bed and return with my luggage. You place it next to the bed, where I can easily reach it.

I unzip my bag and move items around inside. You are standing there watching me. You have no reason to be standing, but you do not sit.

You know what's in the bag, and you are waiting there, like

a child waiting for permission to open her gifts on Christmas morning. Except you know what this present is, don't you?

I purchased your collar almost two years ago. But our relationship made one of its many transitions, a transition toward something platonic in behavior, and away from kink and sex, shortly after.

I moved the collar with me from San Francisco to Chicago, from Chicago to Brooklyn, and from Brooklyn to San Francisco. I took it out sometimes and played with the O-rings on it. I envisioned using them to pull you, to put you in place, where I want you. I thought of pulling on them while I fuck you, choking you while you are on all fours. I waited, patiently, for months and months, for a time when I would place it around your neck.

I waited for now.

I remove it from my luggage. "It's in its own special bag," you tell me, observant, glowing. It *is* in its own special bag, while other items share bags: My harness is coupled with my dick and a glass anal toy; the condoms are with the Hitachi.

Sitting on your bed, I tell you, by patting the spot on the bed next to me, to come and sit. You do.

I get behind you. I place my arms over and in front of you, and down to your neck level, an edge of the collar in each of my hands. I fasten the collar around your neck. I slip my fingers between the collar and your skin: I want to make sure it's roomy enough without being loose. I ask you if it's too tight. You tell me it's perfect.

Still behind you, I grab one of the O-rings and pull your head down to the pillows. You are on your back now, and I climb atop of you again, a knee on either side of your hips. I am sitting up looking down at you.

"I want you to be mean to me," you tell me.

* * *

Last time, it was on the fly. I was naked but for my harness and cock, sitting on the edge of a bed in the historic wing of San Francisco's Westin St. Francis hotel. You were topless and on your knees in front of me. You moved your head up and down my cock. I placed my hand on your head and played with your hair. It was getting a little long, long enough for me to be able to pull it: the perfect length for a butch cut. I played with your hair gently for a short while, and then, deciding breathing was way too easy a task for you to perform, I grabbed your hair tightly, and I rammed your head down.

After a few seconds, you pulled away to catch your breath. Once you did, you returned. You began to lick the head of my cock. You wrapped your lips around it, and I put you through the motions.

You are used to me getting off on your discomfort. And everything that comes with it: hearing how happy you make me; what a good girl you are; how I love to see my little slut's holes filled with my cock; how badly I wish I could shoot cum down your throat while holding your head against me, forcing you to take in the full length of my cock until I'm done force-feeding you my load. That night I did not offer you any such encouragement.

I held your nose, and I shoved deep. You began to gag a few times before you stood up and ran to the bathroom.

I listened to you vomiting. I didn't follow after you.

I was conflicted after that night, but it was a long while before I said anything to you about it. You seemed fine, like you had a good time. I felt silly needing top aftercare, needing reassurance that you wanted it, even though you didn't know it was coming.

It was months before I brought it up, before I told you I had difficulty with the fact it was not planned. I was afraid it had meant I had lost control. You assured me that it actually meant I was quickly shoving my cock in and out of your throat. And that's what happens when I do such things. You quite enjoyed it, you told me.

"I can stop you at any time, you know. You've been worried about this for this long? I will stop you if I need or want to. And, the fact that you think about these things so much? It's just further proof, to me, that I am safe with you."

I get up, and I put on my harness. I fasten my cock inside it. While I'm getting a condom, I tell you I'm going to sit on the chair, the one barely a foot away from the bathroom. You wait for me to sit before you bring a pillow over, place it in front of me, and get on your knees.

I hand you the condom and tell you to put it on me. It's a banana condom. You hate banana condoms, and I packed them for just that reason. You'll suck on it, but you won't like it, nor me. I'm not asking for you to like anything.

"With my mouth?" you ask me.

"Yes, put it on with your mouth." You know I do not like when you use your hands while you blow me. I want to be able to see how much of my cock is in your mouth at all times.

When you begin, you are slow. You suck on my head. You lick it. You lick me from my shaft up; you pause to look up at my eyes. You've told me that the look on my face at this time is always the same—it always says, *this is good, for now.* You swallow more and more of my cock. I keep my hands to myself. I want you warmed up before I start controlling your head movements.

You insert my entire cock into your mouth on your own. I can see none of it when I look down at you.

You are showing off for me, and you start to gag in the process. I think it's time I offered my assistance; I place my hand on your head. I wait for the next time your lips touch the base of my dick, and I hold you there. Just for a little while, and then I let you go. I do this a few times. And then I hold you for longer. I ignore your signs of discomfort: your face is red; your eyes open wide or close tight; I can hear your reflexes going into action.

You place your hand on my cock along with your lips now. Your gag reflex is giving in. You are going to move soon, or you are going to vomit on the floor, which is more than you signed up for.

I let you go, and I remain seated. You keep the bathroom door open because you have no time to close it. I listen to you vomit, and then to the flush. You take a few moments to get yourself together, and you crawl back to me. You wrap your lips around my cock again.

I become more forceful. You are back at the toilet in no time. This time I follow you. It's time to strip away the dignity you kept when you were without an audience. This time—after you flush—you place your head on the toilet paper holder inches away from the toilet seat. I stand behind you.

Something in you has changed. You are not returning to me as you did last time. You are not moving at all. Instead, you wait there, for instruction. I can sense that you are no longer going to act without being explicitly told to. You have entered a place in submission where you cease to make any decision for yourself. You get what game we are playing now: this is not going to end until you fully surrender.

"Get back here. You're not done." I pull you back to me by your collar. You have never felt this light. I can't tell you if it is your submission that makes you lighter, or if it is a peak in my dominance that makes me stronger. I suspect it is a little of both, that you push as I pull. But right now you let me take the credit—you let me feel powerful.

There is always a moment that strikes like lightning when I am suddenly flying. When our energies have created winds strong enough to push us to our opposing sides of the dominant-submissive scale.

This is that moment.

I look at you, and I check in. "Are you okay?" I want to know before I bring this home. You look up at me, and you nod. *Bring it.*

The third and final time you don't flush. You rest your head down on the toilet seat, and you don't move.

I come over to you and place my hand between your legs. Your juices run down my fingers and past my wrist. "You like this, you dirty fucking whore."

"Of course you do," I add. "I'm done with you now. Get cleaned up."

You slowly stand and walk toward the sink, the only other thing in this small half-bath besides the toilet. I see you begin to brush your teeth with toothpaste and your finger, and I tell you that I'm going to get your toothbrush from the other bathroom. I hurry there and back.

I give you your toothbrush.

I get on my knees to clean up the mess.

A PUBLIC
SPECTACLE

D. L. King

Janice, enter the circle of light and disrobe."

Janice walks into the spotlight. It isn't very bright, but since the rest of the room is fairly dark, it serves to make her the focus of attention. She's nondescript. You might call her "medium"—medium height, medium-to-slightly-heavy weight, medium brown hair of a medium length. Her age is indeterminate—somewhere between twenty-five and thirty-nine. Medium age. Her clothes aren't flashy. Actually, she looks like she has come to the spotlight directly from teaching a tenth-grade English class.

She obeys. She steps out of her low-heeled brown pumps and places them against the wall, out of the circle of light. Reaching behind her, she unzips her summer-weight cotton print knee-length dress and steps out of it. She folds it and places it with her shoes. She steps out of her white nylon half-slip and is left in her white cotton nondescript bra and the seemingly out-of-character black cotton thong. The slip goes the way of the dress and shoes. She stops and turns to the sound of my voice.

"Bra, Janice. Leave the panties on."

Looking straight ahead, she swallows. She can hear the watchers but can't see them, in the circle of light, as she is. Janice reaches behind her back, unhooks her bra, slips it off her shoulders, and pulls it away from her body. She tosses it in the general direction of her other clothes and stands with her hands clasped in front of her.

"Careless. Place the bra neatly with the rest of your clothing."

Janice walks out of the light, then returns. Once again, she stands as before. Her breasts are not large, but they are large enough to sag just a bit. Her waist is a little thicker than it appears in clothes, and her thighs rub together just below her sex. The dim light picks up the shadows of a few bruises, one on her thigh and another on the side of her breast.

I love her breasts—the feel of them in my hands.

"Come here, Janice."

Once again, Janice walks out of the circle of light and over to me. I buckle on her leather wrist and ankle cuffs, the heavy ones with the steel rings, and then I hold up her heavy leather collar. It matches her cuffs and has the same utilitarian steel ring. Janice opens her mouth and licks her lips. She nods slightly, giving her assent, and I buckle the collar around her neck.

After her collar is fastened, I let my hands trail down her shoulders and arms. I feel her shiver slightly. Her eyes begin to lose focus, but only for a moment. The act of fastening my collar around her neck always has that effect on her.

"Ready?" Janice nods her little nod. "Climb up on the horse, girl."

My girl walks back into the light and, rather indelicately, climbs onto the black leather spanking horse in the center of the spotlight. She rests her feet and hands on leather-covered bars that run down the sides of the horse, for her comfort. I follow her into the spot and clip one ankle to a ring on the side of the horse and move up toward her head. I clip her wrist, then make my way around the front of her and follow suit with her other wrist and ankle.

I pause to admire her spread cheeks, with the black thong bisecting them, bottom slightly raised. I run my hand over an ass cheek and slide a finger under the T at the top of the thong, bringing it down all the way to the mound of her pussy, but no farther. I slide my finger back up and smooth the thong back against her spread cheeks. I give one a little smack. Working my way back up again, I take a handful of hair and lift her head, enabling me to attach the snap hook to her collar, and then to the ring at the head of the horse. "Make me proud," I say—only for her ears.

It's at this point, when I finish fastening her to whatever piece of furniture I wish to start with, I feel the low buzz of electricity. It starts in my chest and begins to spread. It spreads up to my head and down to my clit and puts me in the proper frame of mind for the game ahead.

My girl is beautiful in her submission. Fastened, as she is, in this posture, she is the most beautiful girl in the world. She will be even more beautiful and desirable as we go on. I can sense people around us. I know they have felt the transformation too. They have seen the plain Jane you wouldn't look twice at on the street transformed into an object of desire. As her submission deepens, she will become even more desirable, and I will become even more desirous of her.

There's something about public play that does it for me. When I hear the watchers breathing, becoming a bit restless, waiting for my play to begin, my feeling of power jumps to the next level. I know once I get started, I will cease to notice the crowd, but for now, for the beginning, it's a powerful aphrodisiac.

I walk out of the light, to the bench where my toy bag waits. Something to wake up the skin. Something easy. The suede flogger.

I run it between her legs, following the curve of her bottom, and over her back, and hear a gentle sigh. The sigh is only for me. It is not loud enough for the others. I work her back, flogging her over and over, and slowly make my way down to her buttocks. I have a rhythm going and it stays constant. Down the back, over the ass, down the thigh, back over the buttocks, down the other thigh, back over the buttocks, and up the back. Over and over. The same rhythm and pattern. Her flesh is awake now; it tingles. If we were home, in better light, you could see an obvious rosy glow, a happy glow. This light is dim. Are you awake, girl? I am.

Enough with the flogger. I switch to the crop. Time to tenderize. I begin gently—slowly. She doesn't make a sound. The only sound is the leather of the crop slapping her ass. The smacks begin to sting. I can tell by the sound. I am not yet breaking a sweat, but she is. I can smell her.

Putting the crop away, I come back to her. Run my hand down her punished ass—between the separation—over the panties. They're wet. Good girl.

"Good girl."

The leather strap hurts her. I love the leather strap. The sound it makes is clean, sharp. Even in this light, I can see the stripes I lay on her ass. Each time I make contact, her ass jumps a bit, but she doesn't make a sound. One final smack—this one produces a yelp. That's all—one yelp. I check on her. Quietly, "Everything as it should be?"

"Mmmmm," she says.

Slowly walking back to her rear, I run my fingers over the welts I've raised. Little juices begin to tease my cunt lips. My arousal is not for public consumption—hers is. Ah, but I am definitely aroused.

If I let her come, if I give her permission, she can climax. She can climax over and over—if I let her. She is not to that point yet. We have plenty of time.

I use my palm to smack her bottom. It won't do to let her cool down now. I scratch her welts and feel her respiration speed up. She is covered in a thin sheen of sweat. Neither of us has entered that particular headspace we strive for yet. I walk back to my bag and return the strap and pull out the heavy leather flogger.

It isn't as gentle as the suede one. It falls hard. I use it on her back, between her shoulder blades. The hits land harder and harder. The rhythm and the strength it takes to wield this tool become an aerobic workout for me. Now I begin to sweat. My breath speeds with hers. I begin to lose myself with each impact. It's a continuous responsibility to make sure I don't completely lose myself to the flow of power.

I don't want to damage her.

I do want to hurt her.

This is as much for her as it is for me. If she doesn't hurt, if there's no true pain, she can't lose herself, either. There would be no point if I couldn't control her pleasure in that way.

I feel the watchers getting restless. She is squirming slightly. I notice her hands clenching and unclenching. I ease up. "What is the word, girl?"

"Green, greengreengreengreen."

"Good girl."

I put the flogger away and take out a thin, whippy cane and slice it through the air. It whistles. I hear the intake of breath and begin on her upturned bottom. Tap tap tap tap tap tap tap. Across both cheeks, over and over in the same spot, gently—tap

tap tap tap tap tap TAP. Her ass jumps several inches above the horse. Tap tap tap tap tap. I smooth the skin with my hand. Gently now, on her upper thighs, tap tap tap tap tap tap. The sound is mesmerizing to me. The feeling is becoming mesmerizing to her. Tap tap tap tap tap tap tap TAP TAP. Shriek. Mmmm, good girl.

I can hear people speaking quietly as I walk back to my bag and exchange the thin cane for a heavier one and walk back to her head. I bend down to check on her. Her eyes are open and unfocused. Her mouth is open.

"Good girl."

I rub the cane against her thighs, then CRACK. Again, slightly lower, I rub it against her skin, then CRACK. Three more times, each a fraction of an inch lower. Each time she jumps. I return the cane. Now I gently run my hand over her bottom and each thigh, smoothing the skin, caressing the welts, putting out the fire. We're both sweating. I run my hand over her panty-clad crotch and it is soaked through. It's time.

I move to the front and pick her head up by her hair again, staring into her eyes. She tries to focus on me. I know she can't. "Now," I whisper, and I watch the orgasm take her. She shivers and shakes almost imperceptibly against the horse, like the shiver that runs up a dog's back when you rub him just the right way. Watching her come like that makes me want to fuck her, drag her off the horse and fuck her on the floor. But we're in public.

We've been playing over an hour. Time ceases to exist. I unhook her wrists and move to her feet to unhook her ankles. I lift her feet off the blocks and they hang limply down, on either side of the horse. Her hands are now hanging in the same way. As I unhook her neck I maintain positive contact with her. Her skin feels electric to me. It feeds the sparks jumping on my fingers.

I help her off the horse and embrace her. She can't stand on her own yet. I slowly walk her to the wall and hook her wrist cuffs to chains hanging from the ceiling, arms outspread. The chains support her. I place her feet apart and hook her ankles to rings in the floor. Now she can rest while I put my toys away. She is positioned facing the watchers, but I don't think she sees them. Oh, she knows they're there, but she is too far gone to be aware of anything other than her own body and me.

We are not done. We will continue. If I can't fuck her now, I'll keep myself on edge until I can. I cup her breast; she moans. I kiss her lips and she attempts to devour my mouth. People come and go. We have hours to play yet, my beautiful girl and I.

THE KEYS

Anna Watson

Maggie almost refused to go into the seedy aquatic park, wanting to sit in the sun and read her book instead, but the kids begged and Stan gave her one of his pleading looks. Once inside, she was startled to see that there were skinny stray cats everywhere, sitting dazed in the sunlight, padding through the greenery. A small, tattered sign said that the park doubled as a refuge for unwanted pets; Maggie folded up a dollar and let Jake, her five-year-old, push it into the metal donation box.

The dolphin show was about to begin, and Stan hustled them along the path, acting like he knew exactly where to go. Ella, teetering on the brink of puberty at eleven, held his hand, clutching her notebook in the other. *Harriet the Spy* had made a great impression on her, and although Maggie swore she would never do it, she had flipped through the notebook once or twice when Ella was asleep.

"Stan and Maggie never talk about anything but us," Ella wrote in her neat cursive. "They must have run out of other things to say a long time ago. I will never get married; I will be too busy with other things."

It was hot in the bleachers, but Jake crawled onto Maggie's lap and huddled there. Anxious boy, he was probably frightened of the water, but his eyes grew wide and sparkly when the trainer had the dolphins dance on their tails to show off their belly buttons. The trainer, hard-bodied and lean in her red one-piece Speedo, had a compelling grin, but mostly looked slightly put upon when the dolphins, two of whom were young and new, couldn't always do what was asked of them.

The trainer was just the kind of woman Maggie was always drawn to, and she found herself watching her face rather than the dolphins, the way her eyebrows quirked, how she narrowed her eyes as she cajoled and commanded, the quick burst of laughter when one dolphin, misunderstanding the command, reared up and kissed her cheek instead of catching the ring on his nose.

Later, standing in line for hot dogs while Stan and the kids watched the sea lion show, Maggie saw the trainer talking with some friends. She could hear snatches of the conversation; they were making plans to go out later that night, the place at mile marker 24. She pretended, even to herself, not to be listening, but she memorized every detail: the way the trainer was standing, insolent and lanky with a towel wrapped around her waist, the way she was flirting with a petite blonde. The trainer looked up and caught Maggie watching, and Maggie turned away quickly, glad she'd just touched up her lipstick in the bathroom.

That night, after everyone but Maggie had fallen asleep watching *The Lion King*, she kissed the kids and pulled sheets over them. Stan was curled in the middle of the other double bed, taking up all the room as if he knew she wouldn't be joining him. They were on an anniversary trip, paid for and arranged by Stan's parents, who had visited the Keys twenty-five years ago and had such fond memories: the vistas, the snorkeling! Things had changed, though, and so far, Maggie had mostly seen a lot of Good Deals, fleets of diesel trucks, dead possums on the side of the road, and once, a tipped-over crate of half-ripe tomatoes rotting in the sun. There were run-down motels everywhere with cute '50s names—the one where they were staying, for example, was called Inn to Your Dreams.

Maggie watched her husband sleeping, feeling the familiar fatigue. Even asleep, he looked unsatisfied and sad. She slipped into the bathroom, where she changed into a low-cut tank top and her island skirt: long, flowing, patterned with red hibiscus. Her mind idled in neutral and she hummed to herself. This wasn't the first time, but that didn't mean she needed to think about it too hard.

The mile markers were almost invisible in the dark, and Maggie had to watch closely. She almost missed the turn, screeching around the corner with a spray of gravel and a long horn hoot from the guy who had been tailing her. Trembling a little, she pulled into a parking place at the back of a square, dusty white stucco building. A neon sign spelled out *The Sea Urchin: Your Favorite Dive*. Maggie sat still for a moment, nervous but relieved to have made it. She got herself out of the car, unsticking her skirt from her sweaty thighs. Resolutely putting her brain back into neutral, she yanked open the door.

All week, she had been sneering at the prevalent descriptor in the Keys of "a little piece of paradise" for everything from a breakfast muffin to the moldy aquatic park where her family had just spent the day. The epithet fit the Sea Urchin, though, and Maggie sighed and smiled, relaxing into the air-conditioning and looking around with pleasure. An island dyke with blonde spiky hair stood behind the bar, a discreet pattern of tropical flowers on her button-down shirt. She glanced at Maggie, sizing her up, eyebrows lifted.

"He'p you?"

So she wasn't even from here; that sounded like a Georgia accent. As a child, Maggie's pediatrician had been a very stern, handsome woman from Georgia, and hearing a Georgia accent still gave her that delicious thrill of desire and dread. Maggie sashayed her way to the bar, leaned over close, and said quietly, "Something cold. You decide. Oh, just as long as there's no damn key lime in it."

The bartender flicked her eyes over Maggie's cleavage, laughed, and set about fixing a drink, flexing her shoulders and making her muscles stand out. Maggie settled herself on the stool and checked out the rest of the place in the mirror. A few clusters of women, a couple of gay guys kissing—it wasn't too crowded yet, and she didn't see the gang from the aquatic park.

"Here it is, darlin'." The barkeep was now in full flirting mode, uncertainty dispelled. "Specialty of the house: a Sea Urchin."

Maggie smiled, paid, and took a sip, watching the bartender swagger off to another customer. The drink was tart and had a zing; just right for such a hot evening. Brain in idle, Maggie scanned the bar again. Ten minutes later, the door banged open and the trainer arrived.

Wearing mirror shades, leather pants, and a white T-shirt, the trainer was far from the sporty dyke Maggie had taken her for at the aquatic park. She looked incredibly butchy, incredibly hot. Feeling nervous again, Maggie blushed as the trainer gave her the once-over. Probably she didn't recognize her, though. Maggie found that usually a woman with kids was invisible to lesbians. Maggie took out her lipstick case and refreshed her lipstick, smoothing the deep burgundy over her thin, expressive lips. When she snapped the case shut and checked the mirror behind the bar, the trainer was still looking. Maggie sipped her drink, adding a fresh kiss to the rim of the glass, holding the trainer's eyes.

Maggie was the first to look away. Stomach in knots, she slipped slowly off the bar stool. Ever since she'd gotten here, she'd really had to pee. Maybe when she got back from the bathroom she would muster the nerve to ask the trainer to dance; some people had started dancing over by the jukebox. She was so intent on getting to the bathroom that she didn't notice the trainer following her. Like a little girl, Maggie began bunching up her skirt before she even reached the stall. Suddenly she felt heavy hands on her shoulders as the trainer came up behind her. Maggie squeaked and half turned, letting her skirt drop.

"Pick that back up and turn around." The trainer had a high, smooth, authoritative voice. Her hands on Maggie's shoulders were firm, commanding. Maggie reached down slowly and slid the skirt back up over her calves, her thighs. She was sweating; the bathroom wasn't air-conditioned.

"The whole thing."

Oh, what am I doing? thought Maggie. Something about the way the trainer was talking to her, she couldn't help herself; she gathered the skirt and pulled it up around her waist, her heart pounding, her pussy coming alive. The last time she had gone out on her own like this, a gentle tomboy had taken her to a hotel and they had spent hours kissing and licking and cuddling. That's what she had been expecting, that's what she wanted. The trainer's hands moved down to Maggie's ass cheeks, sliding the silky material of her panties around and around, roughly massaging, grabbing handfuls of flesh. Maggie was panting, pressing back into those demanding hands. Stan had asked her once how she was able to let strangers touch her, but the trainer seemed to know exactly who Maggie was.

She leaned forward and hissed in Maggie's ear, "You wanted me to follow you."

"No! I mean, maybe, I mean, I don't know!"

The trainer barked out a sharp laugh. "See, I think you're one of these slutty girls who likes to give her husband the slip and come find someone who knows just what she needs. Find someone like me who knows a thing or two about slutty girls like you."

So she did recognize her. Maggie blushed and stammered, trembling with urgency. No one had called her a girl since high school.

The trainer squeezed her ass hard enough to really hurt, and Maggie jumped. "Am I right?"

"Yes, yes!" The answer came tearing out of her.

"And you want me to stay? You want me to stay in here with you, nasty, dirty girl? There's no telling what I'll do, only that I'll do what I like. You'd better think about it."

Maggie had been thinking about the trainer all day. "Stay!" She tried to turn around, but the trainer stopped her, murmuring, "Keep your skirt up."

Maggie rucked it up again, then whispered, blushing, "Please, I really, I have to pee!"

"You have to pee?" The trainer left off ravaging her ass, splayed one hand across her lower belly and cupped her pussy with the other. She squeezed Maggie's pussy, squeezed Maggie's belly, then let go and gave her a push. "Let's go."

Dizzy, confused by sensations—the urgency to pee, the heat and wet in her cunt—Maggie stumbled into a stall and the trainer locked the door behind them.

"Straddle it."

Maggie, her skirt clutched in both hands, got her legs around the sides of the toilet. She was off balance, and the trainer held her waist, steadying her, making her melt. "Now," said the trainer, her hand cupping Maggie's pussy again, squeezing, probing. "Go on."

"I... What?"

"You heard me." The trainer's voice was hard. "You have to pee, so pee."

To distract herself from having to think about this command, Maggie ground her pussy into the trainer's hand, her breath coming hard. She wanted to hold on to the wall, but didn't dare drop her skirt to reach out a hand. She wanted to obey the trainer, whose commands were turning her on so unexpectedly, but how could she? She'd never been into the whole golden shower thing, she wasn't prepared for anything like this, and she really, really had to go.

"I'm waiting."

"My panties—should I...?"

"Leave your panties where they are."

Maggie squeezed her eyes shut. She was going to do it, she knew she was, she wanted to please the trainer more than she'd ever wanted to please any lover. Filled with intense embarrassment, Maggie tried, hesitantly, slowly; then finally letting go, she did it, she pissed through her panties into the trainer's hand, wetting her thighs and the seat of the toilet, splashing everywhere.

The trainer drew in her breath with pleasure as her hand filled and overflowed. "Yeah, you're just as slutty and nasty as I thought," she told Maggie, making her gasp as she shoved aside the sodden material of her panties and found her sopping slit and hole, filling her suddenly with two fingers. Pee was still trickling out of her. The trainer leaned against the stall door and pulled Maggie against her as Maggie's knees buckled. Maggie moved, trying to get a rhythm going, fucking the trainer's fingers, but just as it was starting to get really good, the trainer moved her hand away and began to manhandle her tits, tugging hard at the nipples through her tank top, smearing them with her piss-wet palm. Maggie groaned, trying to keep her skirt up, her wet panties clammy against her hot pussy, and then the trainer grabbed her arms and slammed her hands down on the toilet seat. Maggie got a good grip on the wet seat, instinctively presenting her ass. The trainer pushed Maggie's skirt aside and pulled her panties down to her knees.

"Stay like that." Maggie heard the jingle of a belt and the soft pops of jeans being unbuttoned. The incongruous tearing sound of a condom wrapper. Maggie lowered her head, trying not to let her hair dip into the toilet bowl, wantonly jutting her naked ass toward the trainer, and then the trainer was helping, rocking her, positioning her, and Maggie felt the tip of a dick in her hole. She had never been with a woman who had a dick. She moaned, up on her toes, pushing back.

"Now how about that," the trainer said, grunting with effort, breath ragged. "Mrs. Tourist, up here in the filthy bathroom of the local dyke bar getting her booty fix. Isn't that what you wanted when you first saw me today? You said to yourself, I want that butch's big, hard cock to plow the shit out of me, didn't you, slut?"

The words drove Maggie to the edge, dirty and thrilling, but she shouldn't come yet, should she? She didn't know what to say, could barely form words.

"I asked you a question!" The trainer wound a fist in her hair and yanked her head back, thrusting hard, faster.

"Oh!" Tears came to Maggie's eyes. "Yes!" She was meeting the trainer's thrusts and she felt sexy, so sexy.

"And now what do you want, little wifey? Do you want to

come for me? Are you going to come for me just like you pissed for me, just like you're taking my dick so nice and deep, are you ready to give it up for me like you know you need to, right when I tell you?"

Maggie, her face burning, whispered, "Please, yes, please..."

The trainer snugged Maggie better onto her dick, slowing down, grinding against her ass in long, delicious circles. "Aw, isn't that sweet? This nasty, slutty, pissy bathroom whore wants to come for me. Well, girl, you'd better do it quick, I hear someone opening the door."

Maggie gasped and shook her head no—how could she come with someone else there?—but the trainer was pumping hard again, reaching around for her swollen clit, muttering, "Now, now, now, bitch, now!" and there was nothing for it but to let go again and come huffing and squealing with her forehead pressed against the hard tiles of the wall, barely missing banging her teeth on the plumbing.

The trainer continued to grind into her, grunting and panting through her own come, then she pulled out, slapping her dick on Maggie's ass. There were footsteps and someone went into the stall beside them; they could hear her unzipping her pants. Maggie tried to turn around to face the trainer, starting to giggle nervously, but the trainer held her where she was until the other woman left the bathroom.

"I'm leaving now," said the trainer, still not letting Maggie turn around. "Stay facing the wall until you hear the door shut. You get yourself cleaned up and then come back out into the bar. Oh. You won't be needing these." She stripped off Maggie's reeking panties and dangled them in front of her face, snatching them back when Maggie reached for them. "One last thing: you say, 'Thank you, Sir.'"

"Thank you, Sir!" It came out so heartfelt, the trainer

chuckled. She smoothed Maggie's hair and whispered, "Good girl." Tears sprang to Maggie's eyes, and then she could hear the trainer unlocking the stall door, running water in the sink, and finally leaving the bathroom. The whole time, Maggie stood stock still as she'd been told, holding onto the wall with one hand for support, reading the same bits of graffiti over and over again: "I love Michelle!" "What makes your pussy wet?" "Nipple clamps." "Her tongue." "Xena."

When she heard the door close, she staggered over to the sink and did what she could to make herself presentable.

It was a lot more crowded in the bar now, and no one seemed to be leering at her as she came back into the front room, although she felt incredibly conspicuous. She looked a bit hysterically for the trainer but couldn't see her anywhere. The barkeep waved her over and cleared a spot for her at the bar.

"Here you go, darlin'," she said, reaching for a glass. "Your friend left this for you before she took off." The bartender set a Sea Urchin in front of Maggie with a flourish and a wink. "Said somethin' as to how you might be feelin' thirsty."

COMING
OF AGE

Dilo Keith

Right on time, the doorbell rang. I told my collared sub Brandi to remain kneeling while I answered it myself. Chloe was more fetching than I remembered from our first meeting. She was short, blonde, and curvy, my preferred body type. Not that her shape mattered much, since it was her obedience I sought, but there was no reason I couldn't have it all. The fact that this would be her second time playing—the first with me—could have been daunting for either of us, but she had studied numerous written resources and seemed to have an excellent grasp of the basics. Chloe's first time hadn't amounted to much, according to her; now she wanted the "real thing." She had given me reason to believe I wouldn't have to take baby steps with her, and I intended to make her eighteenth birthday memorable. Technically, we were a week late, a triviality to me, but a source of frustration for a budding slut eager to make her debut.

I had told her to wear something sexy but street legal, with proper undergarments; luscious breasts like hers should be supported and tastefully framed. They were more than a handful, but not out of proportion for her body. The absence of my favorite color in her monochromatic outfit—a black velvet skirt, stockings, high-heeled pumps, and a clingy, low-cut T-shirt peeking out from behind her leather jacket—was disappointing. I had made sure she knew how much I liked blue, particularly a rich hue, like sapphire.

She noticed my lukewarm assessment and took a deep breath before hesitantly asking, "Am I dressed okay?"

"Move the coat."

She spread her leather jacket open.

"That will do." I motioned my girl over to take her coat.

Chloe eyed Brandi but didn't ask for an introduction. Points for her.

As Chloe shrugged out of the jacket, I caught a glimpse of a brilliant blue bra. I amended my previous statement. "You look lovely." There was no need to tell her how pleased I was.

"Thank you...ma'am?"

My almost-butch outfit probably confused her. Black 501 jeans, a silk button-front shirt, leather vest, and soft leather boots complemented my slender build. Well-fitting, comfortable clothes usually gave me a masculine appearance, as did my short, easy-care haircut.

"Ma'am is correct." To be honest, "ma'am" sometimes made me feel old. She was about a third of my age.

While Brandi took care of some preparations, Chloe and I discussed limits, fine-tuning what we had covered in e-mails and phone conversations. Chloe didn't have much to add other than asking if she could make requests. I explained that polite requests and some begging were acceptable. She didn't ask about role definitions, so I brought up the topic.

"I want to be sure we share an understanding about our

respective roles. Brandi is my submissive. The term 'slave' doesn't really fit, although she's as close to a slave as I'll have. Even though you and I haven't established such a relationship, I expect the same obedience. You're obviously intending to submit to me, but you don't belong to me. I also don't think you're seeking a master or owner now."

"What if I *am* seeking an owner?"

"You'll be disappointed." She never indicated in her e-mails that she was the type seeking a mistress to insert into a fantasy of being owned. In case I was wrong, I needed to nip that in the bud.

Chloe pressed her lips together, not quite frowning.

"Why does that bother you?"

"Maybe it's only terminology, but I thought this was more than just bottoming. I want you to use me for whatever you want. Anything safe for me, of course."

"If I decide to tie you to a chair and have you watch me play with Brandi, what then?"

"Then I watch. However, you said begging was allowed."

I laughed. "Yes, I did. And to be honest, it would be a waste to leave you tied to a chair. The point is that you know it would still be using you." She had expressed little interest in bondage except as an occasional tool in other play, an opinion we shared.

"I understand you want me to obey you and not just use you to give me things I want. If it turns out we both want the same thing, that'll be great, but that's not what this is about."

"Then we agree."

"Oh, I do have a question. Exactly how should I address you?"

"I *told* you 'ma'am' was acceptable."

She pursed her lips again, probably because of both lack of information and the mild rebuke.

"I don't require you to use it at the beginning and end of every sentence or anything like that. Just be polite and use 'Mistress Lynn' or 'ma'am' as it seems appropriate. When in doubt, thank me for something, but be sure you know what."

"Thank you for the instructions, ma'am. What about Brandi?"

"I see no reason for you to address her. If something comes up, her name will suffice."

I led her to the playroom and gave her a moment to look around. Her wide-eyed visual tour of the room suggested she hadn't expected such an elaborate dungeon. In addition to several standard pieces of quality bondage and whipping furniture, there was a queen-sized bed and various movable racks for toys. A rest area included a leather couch and a small table with chairs. Brandi laid out snacks and water bottles while Chloe and I sat at the table.

"Brandi baked you a cake for your birthday."

Chloe looked in Brandi's direction.

"You can thank her later," I told Chloe.

I scooped up a fingerful of frosting and held it near her mouth. "I hope you like chocolate."

Chloe accepted my finger and spent a little longer than necessary sucking off the frosting. She started to follow my finger with her lips when I took it away.

"I see you like to suck on things. I'll keep that in mind. Now, young lady, you're overdressed. Stand up."

She reached for the bottom edge of her shirt.

"Not yet. Turn around, slowly. All the way around. Now the shirt. Skirt."

Chloe removed each specified item, placing them neatly on the chair, and then stood in her lovely blue lace bra and panties, properly awaiting instructions.

"Bra. Put your hands behind you and arch your back."

I brushed the back of my fingers across her nipples. "Do you like it when women suck these?"

Chloe looked down and blushed, just a little. I hadn't expected it to be so easy to get a reaction.

"Look at me. That was a question, which is an order to provide an answer."

"Yes, ma'am."

"Yes, you understand, or yes, you like it?"

"Both." Now she was fully blushing. Oh, yes, she was going to be a lot of fun.

"Hands on the table."

I scooped up more frosting and brought my fingers to her lips again.

It would be a waste to limit her talents to fingers, but anything else would have to wait. I considered letting her feast between Brandi's legs, perhaps after tying Brandi to the bed. I filed that image away for later. Using my other hand to lower Chloe's panties, I caressed her ass as I gathered another dollop of creamy chocolate. While she cleaned my fingers, I reached between her legs.

"My dear, you're soaking wet, and all I've done is feed you some frosting."

She lowered her eyes instead of replying, her cheeks pinking again. I told her to stand, and she started to reach for her panties.

"Don't. Just stand there." I went to get a narrow, rolled leather collar, one made for dogs.

"Hold your hair out of the way." I fastened the collar, saying, "It appears that you can follow orders, so you don't really need this to remind you, do you?"

"Not unless you think I do, ma'am."

"Good answer. Pull up your panties."

I ordered Brandi over and held up a wide collar intended as the evening's replacement for her chain. While it was too bulky for everyday wear, I knew she enjoyed feeling all that leather against her throat. As she knelt at my feet, I exchanged the collar, feeding the small brass lock through the closure and pocketing the key.

I noticed Chloe staring at the lock and, I assumed, its symbolism, since her collar didn't have one. Her gaze remained fixed on my moves as I put similar, but not locked, padded leather cuffs on Brandi's wrists and ankles. Chloe soon wore the same restraints. I placed a towel on a nearby chair.

"Take them off," I said, pointing to her panties. Chloe clearly had obeyed my instructions regarding trimming her pubes—short, but long enough that the hairs wouldn't be rough.

I had Chloe put her hands behind the back of the chair where I joined her cuffs to each other.

"Show me that you can move your shoulders. I don't want them to get stiff in that position."

Chloe complied, but looked concerned. I sent Brandi to wait for me by the Saint Andrew's Cross. Returning my attention to Chloe, I pushed her knees apart and secured her ankles to the chair legs.

As I closed the last fastener, Chloe, with obvious frustration, blurted out, "But I thought you said..."

I looked up at the flustered young woman, silencing her with a look before speaking. "First, it sounds like you're about to complain or argue. I suggest that you don't. Second, I never said that I wouldn't do it."

I stepped back to survey the arrangement before patting her shoulder and walking toward Brandi. I hoped I wasn't pushing Chloe too far. I had to know if she could play the way I wanted, and I didn't think it was necessary to work up to it slowly. Her strong personality would be an asset if she could remain submissive. After I took only two steps, she made a disappointing announcement.

"I should get to know what's going on. This isn't fair."

Her face held determination and possibly a small amount of defiance. My instinct told me she would rise to the occasion, but I might have been moving too quickly. After a few seconds of staring at each other, I put aside my doubts and slapped her face. It wasn't very hard, but a faint handprint appeared and her stunned expression told me it got her attention.

"I'll decide what's fair. I thought you were interested in obeying me. Was I mistaken?"

Even with the surprise, her face still reflected a willfulness that didn't disappear immediately. I waited.

"No, Mistress Lynn. Please forgive me."

"I do." I held the back of my hand near her lips. After only a brief hesitation, she leaned over and reverently kissed it before thanking me for forgiving her. When I reached toward her to retrieve some stray hairs that had fallen over her eyes, she flinched.

"Relax. I'm not going to slap you again." I pushed her hair back in place and put my hands on her shoulders. "Do you trust me?"

She nodded, causing her hair to fall again. This time, she didn't move away when I reached for it.

"I'm going to give some attention to Brandi now. I can assure you that you won't be in this spot all night." I hoped my choice of "spot" over "chair" would send an ominous message.

I attached Brandi to the cross, facing the wall, arms spread and above her head, with her feet spread and fastened to rings in the wooden base.

Brandi resembled a redheaded version of Chloe, beautifully

curved and a little past the heavier side of average weight. She was Chloe's height, about five feet, with lovely pale skin dusted with fine red hairs in the places that weren't entirely smooth. The short, wavy hair on her head echoed the bush at the apex of her legs, an occasional inconvenience I accepted in exchange for the visual appeal. Brandi's breasts were slightly smaller, but still a very generous handful. She and Chloe were going to look lovely tied together.

"Very nice," I said, punctuating my comment with a sharp slap on her perfectly rounded ass. "Wait here."

"As you wish, ma'am."

Brandi didn't see me smile at her remark.

I dragged Chloe in her chair to a position where she could see what I was about to do to Brandi.

"I'm not so cruel that I would leave you over there by yourself." I chuckled and added, "Well, actually, I could be, but I feel generous tonight."

I returned to Brandi and gave her shoulder a little squeeze while stroking her back and ass. I started kneading her bottom, adding a few slaps before moving away to pick up a leather flogger. As I gave her a light flogging to build her arousal, her hips moved in the familiar little rocking motion that told me she was getting to a happy place. When I stopped and touched her shoulder, she rubbed her cheek across my fingertips, a signal we developed as a result of playing in noisy clubs. Since I already knew she enjoyed it, the gesture served more as a display of affection. In reply, I kissed the back of her neck before turning her to face me with her back to the cross.

I changed to a rubber flogger made of strands resembling thick, round shoelaces. Brandi calls it my licorice whip. Chloe's widened eyes told me she knew it wasn't for the timid. I hadn't told her very much about Brandi being a pain slut, knowing it would become obvious. Even with my gentle warmup, her skin reddened quickly and her chest, hips, groin, and thighs soon bore marks. Her pale skin and tendency to mark gave the appearance of a severe flogging, judging from Chloe's expression. Wielded equally, rubber often marks more than leather of similar weight. I like rubber for the ease of control, something important when flogging the front of the body.

"Let's make it more interesting. Hold this." I draped the flogger around Chloe's neck and went to the toy table to get a handful of something neither Chloe nor Brandi could see.

"Don't let these fall off."

The objects of attention were miniature plastic clothespins I had already started attaching to Brandi's areolae. Most of her skin wasn't loose enough for the tiny, strong jaws to grasp, but I managed to make a little ring of clips around her nipple. I attached several on her outer labia and put the last few on her ears.

"If you lose any of them, Chloe will feel the consequences. Do you understand?"

Brandi nodded.

I had her repeat the instructions aloud. Chloe looked at me, then Brandi, and back again, her brow knitted.

"Is there a problem?"

After Chloe assured me there wasn't, I resumed the flogging, carefully working around the clips. If they fell off, I wanted it to be because Brandi moved too much, which she eventually did when a particularly hard stroke caused her to twist away. Even aroused as she was, the light clattering sound of clips hitting the ground captured her full attention. She tried to apologize to both of us.

"Don't."

I brought the four clothespins to Chloe. She inhaled quickly as she felt the little jaws bite into her delicate skin, but otherwise remained silent. Each breast now sported a pair of clips.

I returned to Brandi and gave her a few more lashes before removing the remaining clips, watching her face for reactions to the tiny bursts of pain that usually accompany the decompression of the flesh. That sort of pain wasn't her favorite, unlike the flogging, but she accepted it beautifully.

"Shall I kiss it and make it better?" I was removing the clips from her breasts at the time.

"Please, ma'am."

"No talking or noise, now."

I doubted Brandi had time to contemplate why I gave that order before I knelt and sucked her clit into my mouth.

Chloe had managed to be quiet up to that point, but my move elicited a moan and whimper. As I continued sucking on my obediently quiet girl, the intensity of Chloe's needful, plaintive little sounds increased. I stopped after a brief tease, leaving Brandi breathing heavily and pulling at her restraints.

"Is something wrong, Chloe?"

"Please, I...would you..." She stopped and sighed.

"Would I what?"

"Touch me, please." The now-faded sensation of the clothespins biting her breasts was the only stimulation provided since I put her in the chair.

I went over and caressed one breast, knowing the clips' movement would hurt.

She whimpered again, but I thought more from desire for stimulation than pain.

"Aren't I touching you?"

"You are." She looked at the ground.

"She's suddenly become shy. Brandi, you may speak now. What do you think she wants?"

"We haven't delivered her birthday spankings yet?"

"Oh, of course." I put a finger under Chloe's chin and lifted her face toward me.

"Would you like that?"

"Yes, ma'am. Please."

"I told you I would consider requests, and I just gave you a chance to make one. Is asking so difficult?"

"I guess so."

I grasped one of the clips and cupped her breast with my free hand. "This will hurt, but I assume you don't want to keep them."

She nodded and closed her eyes. Despite knowing what to expect, she yelped when the clips released her breasts. After removing her restraints, I took the towel off the chair and put it over my lap as I sat. Pussy trails on black jeans could be sexy, but it was more fun to tease her about making puddles.

I pulled her across my lap and started spanking her hard enough to qualify as spanking, but not something too intense to enjoy. Her gorgeous, squirming, pale bottom showed my pink handprints beautifully. After the first six, I spanked a little harder, and did so again for the remainder. Chloe's adorable ass wriggled appreciatively as I rested my hand on the reddened cheeks.

"There, eighteen."

"And one to grow on," Brandi cheerfully called out.

"Right." I added a particularly hard one.

Brandi called out again, "Ma'am, do I get a turn? It's traditional, you know."

"Girl, you're taking liberties tonight. Do you need to be reminded of your place?"

"No, ma'am. I apologize."

"I accept your apology, but I think you need a reminder.

Chloe will think I haven't trained you very well."

I helped Chloe stand and went to release Brandi from the cross.

"Bring me a cane."

Brandi, who loved the cane, froze in place and looked guiltily at Chloe, who was probably unaware of my intentions.

"Quickly, or the number doubles."

Brandi wasted no time complying.

"Chloe, put your hands on the chair seat and brace yourself."

She looked at my contrite girl, then at me, as if checking that she heard correctly.

"Now."

I delivered one hard stroke and handed the cane to Brandi while Chloe rubbed her bottom. She continued to look surprised. Good.

"After you put that away, if you behave well, you may give Chloe her birthday spanking."

Brandi took her time with the process, caressing the pink bottom draped over her bare legs. I couldn't blame her for lingering on a task I rarely gave her the opportunity to perform, but this wasn't the time for indulgence. I cleared my throat and made the "get on with it" signal with a waggled finger.

Although it wasn't as hard as mine, Brandi delivered a proper spanking. Chloe squirmed on Brandi's thigh, now slippery from her juices. Without pants to protect, Brandi apparently didn't think of using the towel. She had to adjust her grip and Chloe's position more than once to compensate for the slickness. Chloe was so much messier than Brandi, giving me fuel for teasing. When they were finished, Chloe grabbed the towel and quickly swiped it between her legs.

"This will be your last chance for a break for a while. I will admit that I'd happily let you relieve yourself while in bondage, but as I said earlier, I'm feeling generous tonight. Chloe, since you have been losing so much moisture, you might want a sip of water. Not too much, of course."

After their break, I joined my two lovelies with a leather strap around their waists and secured their wrist cuffs to chains hanging from the ceiling. Their bodies lined up beautifully, offset to allow breasts and thighs to alternate and nest together. I went back to using the leather flogger at first, giving Chloe a chance to catch up with Brandi. I didn't stop them when Chloe discreetly tried to hump Brandi's thigh. I hadn't forbidden that, but my girl knew not to seek out her own pleasure without permission and didn't do more than allow Chloe's actions.

When I started using a cane on Brandi, I had Chloe's full attention. The severity of the strokes seemed to surprise her. She leaned her head back to check Brandi's face and appeared satisfied with what she saw. For Chloe, feeling the impact of Brandi's strokes transmitted to her own body must have been very different from merely watching Brandi's whipping on the cross. Chloe closed her eyes when she saw that I was watching her between strokes. Brandi, in contrast, was in her element, moaning appreciatively and happily pressing her body against Chloe with a little wiggle in her hips that I always found so sexy. After ten strokes, I moved into position behind Chloe.

She tensed in anticipation. While excited by some pain, Chloe was clearly not into it like Brandi. I caressed the cheeks still red from the spanking and said, "Relax, or it will hurt more." When she did very little that looked like relaxing, I added, "I'm sure you don't mean to insult me by implying I can't distinguish between your tastes and Brandi's."

She responded by arching her back slightly, presenting the

more delicate parts of her bottom to the cane. I wondered where she learned that.

"Good girl." I laid a carefully calibrated, solid stroke, intending to cause enough pain to excite her without making her suffer. Seeing that it created the desired effect, I gave her five more, with enough time between strokes to create the right amount of anticipation and to allow her to process the sensations. I leaned against her back and collected the juices running down her leg. After slapping her striped ass with my wet hand, I returned to Brandi and rested the cane on her bottom.

"Chloe, pick a number between five and fifteen."

They were notably harder, but Brandi clearly loved all twelve strokes.

"Brandi, you pick for Chloe."

I interrupt them as they exchanged glances.

"No helping." I swatted Chloe. She wisely didn't point out that Brandi was the one trying to help.

Brandi chose half of what she had received, wisely staying safely clear of Chloe's possible limit. I love having smart subs.

"Are you ready?"

Chloe arched her back again and added a little butt wiggle to emphasize her answer. She closed her eyes and leaned her head on Brandi's shoulder to await the cane.

When I finished and had gone to get another toy, I noticed that Chloe was humping Brandi again, which, due to their position, meant she was also pushing into Brandi's crotch. Brandi looked at me, the question obvious in her eyes.

"It's okay this time. You even have permission to come. Slutty Chloe does not."

I dropped my chosen strap and used my hand to spank Brandi until she came with a shout she tried to direct away from Chloe's ear. I helped her stay upright rather than have her wrists bear her weight as she slumped against Chloe.

Reaching around to caress Chloe's face, I said, "Poor baby, all slicked up and no place to go. Be a good girl and we'll take care of you properly. Eventually."

She muttered polite agreement and cooperatively held Brandi while I separated them from the chains and each other. I took them to the bed, in part to assess Brandi's ability to continue. What we had done so far was more like a sampler than a serious scene, and she was ready for more. Chloe, of course, was getting frustrated, something I pretended to ignore.

"You've both behaved well, considering. Each of you may make a specific request. Brandi?"

"Did you bring those new nipple clamps? I would love to try them."

"Chloe?"

"I would be grateful if you would fuck me, ma'am."

"May I change my request?" Brandi asked. I gave her a sharp look. I normally don't mind some playfulness, but I expected her to set a good example.

"I have some answers for you, in order. Yes. What do you think of Brandi doing it? No, and if you continue to be silly, you'll be the one left in the chair." I looked at Chloe. "Answer the question."

"Brandi would be fun, but if I say yes, does that count as my request?"

"Since I'm the one encouraging you to ask, no. Make another request, greedy slut, and you might get both."

"I'd be grateful if you would spank me again, with your hand, and..." She hesitated.

"And?"

"With your clothes off. I wouldn't want to mess them up."

I was impressed with how she delivered her lines with

enough humor to be interesting while staying in her role. She was turning out to be less reticent than I first thought.

"I'll grant part of your request."

I left her to wonder which part I meant while I attached the clover clamps (the ones that get tighter under tension) to Brandi's nipples. An experimental tug on the chain elicited a delicious moan from my girl, so I tried again, this time holding the chain and pushing Brandi away. She loved it.

I turned to Chloe. "Now *you*, slut. That's something I normally wouldn't do at this point, but I like to reward obedience, and I told you to make a request."

Sitting on the edge the bed, I motioned to Brandi. As she knelt across from my feet, I used my booted foot behind the chain to guide her closer. I pressed my foot against her chest, pushing her breasts apart. She moaned in that delightful manner she usually does when I manipulate her body in crude ways.

Brandi removed my boots and helped me shed my jeans. I guided Chloe over my lap and pinned her arms behind her back with one hand. After giving her a thorough and erotic spanking that left her moaning and whimpering, I nudged her legs apart and spread her wet, swollen lips, pausing with a single finger at her entrance.

"Oh, please..." Her request faded into a whimper.

My teasing probe seemed to be worse than doing nothing because she appeared more frustrated.

"You really need to be fucked, don't you, slut?" I added two more fingers.

Squirming on my lap, she moaned and nodded while pushing back against my hand.

"Good."

I rolled her off my lap and onto the floor, where she remained until I instructed her to get on the bed, on her back. She scrambled into place while I wiped off and dressed. As I had instructed with whispered words earlier, Brandi, now equipped with a dick-shaped lavender dildo in a black leather harness, crawled across the bed and stopped by Chloe's feet, awaiting orders.

"Have the Chloe slut suck you. I recall she's good at that."

Brandi positioned her cock over Chloe's mouth and silently checked with me before continuing.

"Do as you like, but no coming, neither of you until you get permission." I knew Brandi's harness hid a buried dildo on the other side.

I sat on the other side of the bed to watch Brandi use her big purple dick on Chloe, first making her suck it so long that I wondered about Brandi's latent sadism. I eventually joined in, holding Chloe's knees by her shoulders while Brandi banged away below. It didn't take long for Chloe to start pleading alternately for permission to touch herself and for release. When relatively proper requests dissolved into frantic begging, I gave them both permission and pressed Chloe into the mattress by her shoulders. Her attempts to thrash around revealed more strength than I had guessed. I thought about suitable bondage for the next time.

As they lay in a sweaty heap, I decided Chloe possessed the makings of a delightful plaything—slutty, easy to tease, and relatively obedient—plus the potential to be more than an infrequent play partner. I didn't want to appear too eager to get her in my dungeon again, but I had the perfect excuse for our next meeting. I gathered them into a hug and stroked Brandi's hair.

"You know, it's Brandi's birthday next month."

NOT WITHOUT PERMISSION

Sinclair Sexsmith

My girl, Kristen, is on her knees on the hardwood floor next to my desk for a full minute before I realize she's not petting the cat or tying her shoe: She wants my attention.

I stop typing and turn toward her slightly. "Yes?"

She hands me her collar, eyes downcast. "It's Tuesday night."

"Yes?" I take the collar from her palms. I know what she wants, but I want to hear her say it.

"You said I could..." She hesitates. "You said I could come tonight."

"I did, huh?"

"Yes." She brings her eyes up to mine, searching: *Didn't I remember?* Of course I did.

"I think I said you would have the *opportunity* to come tonight."

She looks hopeful, grateful.

I finger her collar. "When I put this on, our play starts. You know how it works. Are you ready for that now?"

"Yes, Sir."

I consider. I'm in the middle of a project, but it is getting late. I can wrap this up for tonight. I did promise her the chance, and I like to keep my promises, especially to her. "All right. Give me twenty minutes to finish up, then meet me in the bedroom. Strip, and wait for me on your knees." I fasten her collar, the thin metal hoop with the heart-shaped lock, and pocket the key before cupping her face in both of my hands for a moment, kissing her, sweet and slow and light.

When we pull away, she nods and rises. I watch her go and attempt to turn my mind back to my work, but find myself daydreaming, plotting what I'm going to do, how I'm going to use her sweet body. I want to push her. This will be her first orgasm in almost a week; I want to make it good.

The twenty minutes seems to take two hours, but I manage to send a few e-mails and finish enough that I can leave it for the night. I dig into the toolbox I keep in my office and pick a long cock of medium thickness, good for fucking and sucking, before I go into the bedroom. I wait until the twenty-second minute, because I know she's been on her knees since the eighteenth, and I want her to wait. To want it. To be thankful when she gets it.

When I enter the bedroom, Kristen is facing me with her head down, hands clasped behind her, on her knees on top of a small folded throw blanket. She wears nothing but her collar on her neck and the thin star ring I gave her on her left ring finger. She straightens a little when she hears me approach but does not look up. I grin.

"You look lovely, waiting for me."

"I'm...ready." She swallows.

"I'm sure you are." I finger her hair and run my hands through it. It is past her chin now, baby-fine with a golden shimmer. She leans into me a little. I touch her cheeks and chin and jaw and lips, she parts them to suck one of my fingertips into her mouth. She is turned on already, tongue swollen as she flicks it against the crease in my finger.

I lean in next to her ear. "I'm going to beat you for a little while first. I want to leave some marks on you. If you get to come, I want you to remember who does this to you, who lets you, who makes you feel good. Then I'm going to fuck you—" I haven't decided how yet, I'll figure that out by the time I get there. "If you can make *me* come, pretty girl, you can come after that. But not before. Understand?"

She nods, sucking two of my fingers now.

"Good." I remove my hand and take her black leather ball gag from the top drawer of our tall slender toy dresser. "Since you like something in your mouth so much," I say, and kiss her, tonguing her mouth as she sighs, before I slip the gag in and buckle it behind her head.

She shudders a little and her body relaxes, already giving in. That shudder shoots right through me and I feel sparks climb my spine.

"All right, up," I say, then tug on her elbow when it takes her a moment to register. She scrambles to her feet. I shove her, hard, quickly, to the bare patch of wall next to the closet and pin her there with my body, one hand on the side of her face to press her cheek into the plaster. I hold her there a second and we both breathe.

"Ready?" I ask, at her ear again. She nods. "Hands on the wall."

She reaches as I unbuckle my belt and whip it from the loops of my jeans. She tries to say, "Oh, God," but it comes out as a whimper through the gag. I can hear the syllables, the vowels.

I let my arm be loose, let the leather be soft and supple as I warm up her ass and thighs and back. She gets supple too, her body relaxing and releasing already, muscles easing up their tight grip on her bones. She leans into the wall for support.

I get a little harder and see a thin line of drool start to fall from her mouth and chin. She tries to wipe it with her shoulder but keeps forgetting about it when my belt reconnects and snaps her into the sensation. She breathes deep. I widen my stance. Her back is striped with lines, her ass and thighs red and splotchy. I take a few full-winged swings with my legs spread, back spiraling, pulling up as I feel my cock's extra weight pulling down between my legs. She gasps as it hits, once, then a pause, then twice, then again as I wind up and throw. She collapses a little into the wall on the third and I know she's almost done. I press my body against her sensitive backside and she gasps, arches her spine like a cat, lolls her head back on her neck to rest against me.

She leaves her hands on the wall, never moving them. She must really want to come tonight.

I gently run my hands along the sweet curves of her body, resting on her ass before letting my fingers travel down between her legs.

She is wet, dripping down her thighs.

I touch gently, soft as I can, just the slightest stroke, and she softens, knees buckling, before she jerks up and pulls away from me, twisting her face around to plead with her eyes. With the gag in her mouth she can't tell me, but I can understand her: She'll come if I keep touching her. She is already that close.

I take my hand away and move both up to unbuckle her gag. She moans as it comes out of her mouth and she swallows, wipes her chin on her shoulder, not moving her hands, and manages to say, "Thank you."

I drop the gag. "Turn around, give me your wrists."

She turns and drops her arms in front of her, offers herself to me. I loop the belt around both wrists and pull it tight, then snake the end back through between them so she's locked in handcuffs. I pull on the end of the belt and bring her toward me, bring my arm around her tender back, lightly brushing my hand along her spine as I kiss her mouth, cheek, jaw, neck. I could devour her like this: she is liquid and soft, and holding her, entering her, is like diving underwater.

Little murmurs of pleasure bubble up through her lips and I pull her close to me, delight in the feel of our bodies pressed together. But she's got me all hard, too, and wanting, still edgy, hips tight and ready to buck.

I push her gently. "On the bed."

She lies down face up and scoots back onto the bed. From between her legs I push her wrists above her head with one hand and struggle to rip the button open, get the zipper down on my jeans, to get my cock out. She pushes with her legs against the bed and keeps moving herself back. I slide to keep up with her, and by the time I pull my cock free, she's got her hands against the wall, pushing back against it so I can press into her, and I sit up to grip the tender flesh of her inner thighs as I guide my cock inside her with my hips. It slides in perfectly the first time, her hips wide and open, knees pulling back, and I tear off my T-shirt before dropping down on top of her, thrusting all the way in.

My harness is tight and I feel every inch, every resistance she offers with her tight cunt as my hips thrust against her.

"Fuck, fuck," she cries, wrapping her legs around my waist, gripping me hard, pulling me in deep. I didn't think I was this hard, this ready to burst, but I am, and she's still pushing on the wall so I can pull her harder toward me, my arms wrapped under her, her skin still hot and red where I'd marked her up.

I can't believe she hasn't come yet.

"Come inside me, do it, fuck me, I want you to, please, please..." she starts begging. That little whine in her voice does it for me every time. I cry out, feel my clit pulse and shake against the harness strap, my stomach crunching, ass tight and pressing forward so I can grind against her, harder, thrust in once again, milking the last of the orgasm through my body.

My jeans are tangled over my ankles and I reach down to toss them off, then bring my hands back to her hips, bring the tip of my cock to her hole again. I move one hand to flick her clit, big and pink, with my thumb.

She moans.

"You are so being good, baby," I murmur, sitting back on my heels, knees pushing her thighs apart, cock still just one inch inside her, knuckles against her clit. "You took that very well, and you made me come so quick. You were perfect tonight."

"I was?" She brings her hands down to her chest and I unwrap the belt from her wrists.

"Perfect," I say again, leaning forward so she can wrap her arms around my back, leaving just enough room that I can still rub my hand against her pussy. "Do you think that was good enough for you to come?"

Her eyes flash a little, widen. I can see her thinking, what if I don't let her? What will she do then?

"Yes?"

"Hmm." I move my hips a little and tease her wet hole with my cock. She's tight, still trying not to come. Not without permission. When she is right on the edge, I want to keep her there. I want to train her well enough that she can practically come on command.

"Ohh," she moans. She tears at my shoulders with her perfect manicure. It stings, and I remember the way it looked, so fresh and slick and bright, when she ran her hands all up and down the shaft of my cock last night as she sucked me off on the couch. She has been waiting a long time for this one.

I shove all the way in and rub her clit a little harder. "You've been so good, pretty girl. You waited so well this week. Go ahead, you can come now. Come for me."

That's all she needs, just that flash of permission, and she shakes and comes, and I don't let up but thrust harder and keep with the small circles over her clit. She gasps and slams her arms down onto the bed, back arching, as she comes in rapid succession, two-three-four times, so I pause when I'm all the way inside her, then pull out slow, and she comes again. I almost laugh at how easy it is, at her sensitivity, and sit up again to push her legs by the backs of her knees as I fuck her a little more as she moans, arching my hips up and aiming up for her g-spot, and I only get two-three-four thrusts in before she comes again, this time squirting hard in a stream that gushes and arcs, high enough that I can see it, before her pussy squeezes so tight she pushes my cock right out.

Breathing hard, I collapse next to her. I've lost count. She nestles up against me and brings her hand down to grip my cock, strokes it a little, more like a comforting gesture than an attempt to turn me on. She sighs and we wrap around each other.

"When can my next one be?" she asks after a minute of quiet, as we both get our breath back.

"Perhaps Saturday," I offer, mentally checking my schedule. She nods and gives me that little smile, pushes her hair back from her face, and adjusts her collar around her neck.

"But Tuesday's not over yet," I say, and turn to kiss her beautiful face.

FEATHERS
HAVE WEIGHT

Alysia Angel

I watched you skulking around in the alley where I asked you to meet me. You were so *on time.* I enjoyed how your pacing slowed after a while. You looked at your watch, the sky, your eyes squinting down the alley where I was positioned behind a half wall, unseen in the dark not far from you. I know you well enough to know that you were starting to wonder if I was ever coming, if perhaps something had happened to me en route. You know I always keep my word. I enjoyed watching the concern and love dance across your pretty face.

After a few more minutes, I casually stepped out of my hiding spot, my heels making tiny clicking sounds on the cobblestones. As I approached, you straightened just a hair, the lines of your body like telephone wires, taut and bundled with ropy tension. I stalked around you and hooked a long red nail into the ragtag boy hanky at your throat. Into the cold air, while jerking the fabric hard from away from your neck, I said, "I know puppies that wear hankies around their necks like this," and your whole

face flushed under the dim streetlights. I could see the blush
travel down your fawn neck in fat little red fingers, making my
fangs press insistently against my bottom lip.

 You stood against the wall, your bruiser face on, one boot-
clad foot pressed into the bricks to steady you. I pressed nearer
to you, close enough for you to smell my amber oil, my tits
grazing against your tough-guy leather vest, and you started to
look nervous.

I liked that.

I slowly reached up and pushed my fingers into your short
hair. I smoothed sleekly the back of your skull, the soft bristles
of your hair pressing back into my hands with the eagerness that
you carefully kept off your face. Your head bowed just barely.
It was enough.

My heels kicked at your huge boots with force. You resisted
and looked down at me with a flash of defiance, nostrils flared
and jaw working. I kicked harder. This time higher above the
boot line, and you winced but slowly spread your legs. I let the
crackle of electricity build between us, the smell of the alley damp
and cool around us, the bricks against your back and thighs. My
breath was in the air like mists around your handsomeness. I
reached up languidly and touched your face, and as you softened,
I pulled away quickly and slapped, watching with pleasure as
your head snapped to the side and then slowly back into position. Your pupils were blown open like a dark poppy thrust out
of a crack in the cement. Beautiful, like it just didn't give a fuck.
I slapped you again even harder, enough so I could feel the warm
little prickles jump around on my palm. Your head came up faster
this time, a sneer on your lips, that defiance back in your eyes. I
took that moment to put my hand over your mouth and place my
other hand on your jeans-clad cock, stroking my nails against it,
raking them hard enough for you to shiver in spite of yourself.

"On your knees," I said softly. You hung back and I punched you three times with my small fist in your substantial chest. You slid down to your knees. I enjoyed you there, now lower than me, your boyish face refusing to look up.

I yanked your hair back, forcing your face up, and I said, "Who am I?" Confusion passed across your face like a fog and you responded with "Ma'am?" I slapped you one-two-three with my left hand across that pretty face of yours.

"The proper way to address me tonight is Daddy." Your eyes rolled back in uncomplicated surprise and joy while your red lips formed the words: "Oh. Yes, Daddy." Your mouth was still slightly open, so I took the chance to shove four fingers into it. I took great pleasure in the way your tongue felt against the pads of my fingertips, how my nails scraped against your tenderness.

As I slowly fucked your mouth, I asked you to lift up my vintage dress. With shaky hands you pressed it upward, eyes never leaving mine, and I said in my sweet honey voice, "You can look down, darlin'." You glanced down and your mouth opened wider around my fingers, which slid out of you and into my panties to pull out Mustang.

Mustang shot down your eager throat like a hungry snake and you gagged, sputtering around its girth. Your eyes rolled around like a horse at a track, trying to get out of the gate to win the race.

I pulled out and slapped your face with my cock. "No teeth this time," I said as I alternated cock-slapping you and rubbing the head of my dick across your impossible lips. You looked so hot with your mouth working so hard and your fingers hooked into my fishnets, pressing into my thighs for support.

"You may touch my pussy," I said softly to the top of your beautiful head as it bobbed swiftly up the length of my cock. Your hand wasted no time sliding aside the band of my black lace panties and pressing under my cock against my clit. Your cheeks sucked in hard as your fingers slid easily into my ready hole, two and then three all the way inside me. You moaned and nearly lost your balance as I held on to the bricks for support and leaned back so I could spread my legs further apart. You never stopped sucking my dick as you fucked my pussy hard like you know I like it, your thumb jammed under my cock and on top of my clit. I let you fuck me like that until I came, fast and rapid panting.

"Did you like fucking Daddy like that, boy?" I asked as I glanced down the alley to check our position. You mumbled out a "My God yes, Daddy" around my cock and slowly removed your hand from my pussy.

"Unbuckle your belt, take it off, and face the wall," I said as I regretfully put my dick away. You complied and I came up behind you, lightly punching your back, kicking your legs apart to a position that pleased me and taking the belt out of your right hand. I reached around easily, my tits pressed against you and unbuckled and unzipped your jeans with one deft move. They slid to your knees and I slowly pushed your gay boy underwear down just enough to expose your ass.

My nails dug into your beautiful ass cheeks, leaving matching red marks on either side, and you shivered onto the bricks. You turned your head to look back and I punched you in the back, hard, in rapid succession until you were facing the wall again. You moaned and I smiled a feral smile into the back of your solid body. I marveled over how much taller you were than me as I hit your ass solidly with your own doubled belt. Your body jolted and I hit again, asking you to count for me.

You counted to thirty and I checked in, saying, "Too much, boy?" And you with your gritted teeth hissed out, "No, Daddy," so I hit you harder until I was pleased with the welts that were already spreading across your beautiful ass. I made you stand there in silence while I reached into my bag and pulled out a bottle of water, took some swigs, and then spat in a fine arc all across your red ass. You moaned as the cold air hit the wetness of you, and I slapped it just to make sure you got the point.

"Bend over, boy," I said, maintaining my composure as you bent over, exposing yourself to me with your usual grace. I put my hand between your legs from behind, and with the full intention of shaming you, I commented on how wet and hard you were for me.

"What do you want?" I asked while cupping you. No answer. My left hand came down three times on your massively welted ass and I asked again, more loudly this time, "What do you want, boy?"

While catching yourself in a whimper, you slowly said from your position against the bricks, "I want you to fuck me, Daddy."

And how does a punk boy like you think that he deserves my cock inside him? I pressed my panties-clad hard-on against your asshole, and your boy back shuddered once. "Please, Daddy," you said clearly into the cold air.

I turned you around and pressed my hand on your cock, exposed and slick with excitement. I slid my small fingers along the length of it, looking up into your lusty eyes, and said, "Good boy." I pulled back into myself, patted my hair, and picked up my bag, swaggering down the long alleyway.

You stayed there as instructed, awaiting my next move.

STRONG

Xan West

for A., who said it deserved its own tale

For both of us, gender is both complex identity and elaborate sex toy. But not just that. It is not easy to grow up breaking the gender rules, to live lives visibly nonconforming. Gender is a dangerous and delicious edge in which we play, knowing that we may inadvertently step on the minefields of our gendered histories and present struggles. Part of the thrill is that danger. We push gender to its own edges, play its sharpness against our throats, fear in our mouths, ache in our guts, building armor against becoming what we fear.

Gender is the core. It drives our relationship. As a transgender butch, playing with gender is an edgy and necessary thing. For my genderqueer submissive, whose gender ebbs and flows in life and in play, the conscious choice to play with gender confirms self, breaks boundaries, allows catharsis. My submissive is both my girl and my boy. Tonight she was going to be one and then the other.

When she is my girl, I always start by fucking her throat. It is the most personal hole, and I claim her there first, make sure she knows she is helpless to stop me. Her job is to open to me, give to me, feed me with her eyes. I begin by placing the cuffs on her wrists, locking them together, and forcing her to her knees. My hands grip her hair, and I force her mouth onto my cock. This is how we start, every time.

Beginning this way every time gives us both a way to go deeper into ourselves, to sink into what we are doing, find ground for the genders we are playing in. My cock in her throat honors how she wants to do girlness, how much we both want her to be open and vulnerable and raw. Her eyes looking up at me and her mouth wrapped around my dick reflect back the masculinity I want to do with her, how much we want me to be cruel and invasive and dominant. I need to see that she wants this, all the way through, and she knows how much I run on adrenaline when we play this way, how it reaches into my core and twists.

I need to start fast, and hard, almost dare myself into it, because this scares the shit out of me, and that's the only way to get over the mountain of fear that builds in me as I know we are going there. The more fear there is, the rougher and faster I need it. I was especially rough that night, ignoring the gagging, groaning as I forced tears from her eyes.

"That's right, choke on my cock," I said gruffly.

There was rushing in my ears as I watched her choke, tears streaming down her cheeks, her eyes locked on mine, soft, reassuring. I rammed myself into her, cracking her open, thrusting my way inside. I got taller as I fucked her face, wrenching her hair, relentless. I could tell when she started to float, weightless, rapt. I pulled out of her mouth, looking coldly down at her as she took ragged, sobbing breaths and offered herself to me.

I lifted her up from her knees, unlocked her cuffs, and seated her in the bondage chair, clipping the cuffs to it and attaching her ankles. I put her in this chair when she's a girl. It reminds her to keep her legs spread for me.

It's a rule of mine. When she's my girl, she is required to keep her thighs apart. They never touch in my presence. It makes her constantly aware of her body, the position she's in. She is always conscious of her cunt. I want it to feel exposed, even behind layers of clothing. Exposed just by her own awareness. With this one simple rule, I claim ownership of her body, her cunt, her focus. From across the room I am inside her, spreading her thighs, exposing her cunt, deep inside her head.

The chair is an intensification of the rule. More than that, it takes a private thing and makes it public. I always choose to put her in the chair that faces the crowd, the chair that is the most public. I display her body, spread her thighs for all to see.

It was crowded that night. By the time I had her bound to the chair, there was a circle of voyeurs behind us, devouring her exposure. Dozens of eyes were on her skin. She was trembling. I wanted to intensify the exposure, use their gaze to push her further, ride the wave of that. I pulled out my knife and slid it along her cheek, her throat. I began to cut off her clothes. The knife bared her flesh to the room, ripping through fabric, revealing her as she struggled to remain utterly still, biting her lip, eyes closed. I teased the knife along her thighs, taking advantage of her closed eyes to pull something out of my bag and get it ready. The knife edged its way closer to her cunt. I spread her to it, teasing it against her, and then rammed my baton into her cunt in one stroke, pulling the knife away. She trembled openly, stuffed full, her eyes begging.

"Come for me," I said, pulling her hair.

She did, her body contracting, trying to push the baton out even as I held it there, forcing her to take it. Her eyes were wide and dark. I released her hair and removed the baton, wanting her to be aware she was empty and aching. More than anything, when she is my girl, she needs to be exposed and penetrated, made aware of her cunt and the eyes of others.

"The whole room just saw you come, girl. They know your cunt is dripping, aching to be stuffed full. Their eyes are on you, watching. You can't hide now, girl. We can see you. You are naked to us."

She is so strong. I can't imagine seeking this level of exposure, this level of vulnerability. She awes me.

I pulled out my clover clamps and attached them to her nipples. She hissed when I put them on. I let the chain fall and tugged on it, watching her squirm for me. I wanted her aware of her skin, feeling me penetrate it with pinches and bites. I leaned in to bite her shoulder, tugging the chain, and felt her writhe, her pulse beating under my tongue, my teeth grinding into her.

I lifted my head and placed the chain between her teeth. She would feel a steady, relentless pull on her nipples and have something to bite down on. She was going to need it.

I pulled out my favorite cane. It is rattan, thin and whippy. Her thighs were exposed perfectly for it. This was no slow, even buildup. It was about opening her up, ripping her open, and that was clear from the start. I drove the cane into her, relishing the sounds it forced from her, slicing into her thighs. The more I drove it into her flesh, the larger I grew. This was more than just dominance. When I take my masculinity and rub it against her girlness, I feel gigantic, and she is so fragile in comparison. This is one of the lines we ride with this kind of play, and one of the many risks inherent in it is that it might actually reduce her in her own eyes, or in mine. That I, or she, might actually be unable to see how strong she is. Part of the intensity comes with the risk. At that moment I stepped outside myself just a bit to check in with myself, read her a bit closer, before sinking back into it.

I began to breathe with her, building, ramping up the pain, barely pausing between strokes. I rained fire onto her, purple welts forming. Her eyes were closed tight, her teeth gripping the chain, her face contorted in pain, and she finally began to try to get away. Of course she couldn't. That was the point. She was trapped, her legs spread wide, attached to the chair by ankles and wrists, her cunt exposed to all, and those naked vulnerable sensitive thighs sliced into, relentlessly, no matter what she did. She began to shake her head, not caring about the pain it caused in her nipples. But she did not say her safeword, did not do the one thing in her power that might free her. Then it happened. The invasive pain spilled through her and out her eyes, tears streaming down her face.

"That's right, cry for me. It will only make me want to beat you and fuck you harder, girl."

I struck harder, repeatedly, watching it sink in. That she was helpless, exposed, vulnerable. That I would take it all from her. That she was free to move all the way through it and out the other side. It took me a long time to get her to a place where she was willing to cry. Before me, she had not met a top who didn't stop the second the tears started flowing. She still didn't quite trust it, needed me to show her, again and again, that I would keep going, that she could be that strong, give that much, let me see her tears.

The pain moved through her in waves, pouring out her eyes, and I could see the joy spread over her face. She was beautiful in that moment, and I savored it, pouring pain into her and watching it flow through her, riding that. It was time. I set down the cane and took my cock out of my jeans, pulling on a condom. I slid in slowly, luxuriating in every inch of penetration, watching her eyes. I leaned in and licked the tears from her cheeks as I felt her let go. I began to fuck her, my hips ramming into her sore thighs, making her scream as the chain fell from her mouth.

I growled, "Mine," in her ear as I slammed into her, feeling her body begin to shake as the sensations overwhelmed her. I removed a clamp, ordering her to come for me. She began to sob as she came, my cock driving into her, pain racking her body, her senses on overload. It felt like perfection to claim her.

"Mine," I snarled as I removed the other clamp, watching her body move, struggling against her bonds, tears streaming down her face. I leaned in and bit her as I fucked her, pounding into her with my cock, driving into her with my teeth, opening her up for my pleasure. I growled into her skin as I bit, my hips slamming into her rapidly, my hands fisted in her hair.

She was sobbing loudly, and it felt so damn good to hear it, the sound reaching right down and stroking my cock in a long velvet caress. I lifted my head and grabbed her eyes with mine.

"You are mine. My girl. Come for me, loud."

She began to shudder and moan, her cunt contracting so hard on my cock, tears pouring out of her eyes.

"My girl," I growled as I came, my hands gripping her hair as I spurted inside her cunt. I closed my eyes and held her, just held her for a long time, savoring the feel of being inside her to the hilt. I carefully pulled out and discarded the condom, cleaned her off gently, and gave her some water. I got her down from the chair and brought her over to the couch, seating her at my feet and stroking her hair.

She laid her head on my thigh, holding on tightly to my boot, and trembled for a good long time. Then she was quiet and still, her hands on my boot slowly easing. She lifted her head to look up at me.

"Sir?" she said.

"Yes?"

"May I please clean up the space and go change?"

"You may," I said, smiling, stroking her cheek, and then watching her as she cleaned the chair and then walked away. She once told me, "Being a girl is like being without armor. Sometimes like being without skin, even. Your power is in your vulnerability and openness. Most of the time, girl is not a safe thing to be. That's why I treasure being your girl, it's a safe place to touch that danger and roll around with it. But sometimes, when I'm putting myself together after you rip me open and poke my soft spots, what I really need is armor. That's one of the best times to be your boy." That's what we had planned tonight. He asked specifically for that, said he wanted to walk out tough and strong and wearing his armor.

He moved differently when he was my boy. His center of gravity was lower, and he swaggered. He strutted over to me that night, grinning, stopping to stand crisply before me, hands locked on wrists behind him. I eyed him slowly. He was looking sharp in BDUs, tight enough to show the dick he was packing, black ribbed undershirts three layers deep, and shiny black Corcs, his hair slicked back. I love a boy in an A-line shirt.

"Grab my bag, boy," I said, and stalked off to claim a semi-private space. I found a perfect corner, where the light was dim and there was no equipment. When he's my boy, I want him standing. He's tough. He can hold himself up. I pulled on my leather gloves and backed him into the wall.

"That's it, boy. Just you and me and a wall. Show me how strong you are, boy."

I started steady, pounding him with my fists, going after his muscles. We breathed together, slow and easy. Ramming into his pecs, his biceps. Going after his quads. Rhythmic, even pounding setting the stage. This was about strength, endurance. Mine, and his.

"Show me what you can take, boy. What you're made of."

I slammed him into the wall with my bulk, reminded him that I have a hundred pounds on him. He stuck out his chin, just a bit. I slammed into him again, propelling my weight into him. Again, taking his breath with my girth. Again. His eyes started to get glossy. I stepped back and began to kick. I drove my boots into his thigh muscles, delighting in the sound of him grunting with each blow. I used my knee to strike his thigh, watching his eyes get darker.

Sinking into thud roots me, pulls me deep into myself. Using my whole body helps me reestablish, find my footing. He's not the only one who needs to put himself back together, and he knows it. Knows that this is for both of us, that I need this as much as he does, and his job is to feed the energy back to me, to help keep it cycling between us.

I moved up closer to him, pulled on my SAP gloves, and pounded his pecs. Steady. Repeated. Relentless. Lead shot hammering his chest. Holding his gaze.

"Take it for me, boy."

It was intense for him. I knew it. His breath became more ragged, his jaw clenched. I could see the determination in his eyes. I just kept ramming my fist into him, watching him closely.

He is so strong. I know what it is to endure this, to stay standing through it, to face my own limits and keep pushing them. He awes me.

"That's my boy," I said as I hit him. "Show me how tough you are. Take it for me."

He did. Not a sound. He stood still and took it for me, his

jaw clenched down on it, his hands fisted, frustration clear in his eyes as tears slid down his cheeks. We both ignored them. They were meaningless, as unimportant as the people quietly watching us. What was important was that he stood still and took it, for me. He made me proud, and I let it show in my face.

I pulled out my knife and stroked his throat with it, teased it against his lips, and grinned at the sight of his tongue snaking out to lick the blade, his lips opening to it, his hand slipping up to hold my hand steady, begging in his eyes. I nodded and allowed his hand to clasp over mine, holding the knife, watching his mouth engulf it, his eyes wicked and triumphant. Sucking off a knife takes talent, practice, love, and deep respect for a sharp blade. My boy was very good. It was a delicious sight, and I savored it, groaning, my dick throbbing.

"That's my good boy," I whispered roughly.

I put my hand on his chin and held him, easing the blade out of his mouth, wiping it on his shirt, and putting it away. I pulled out my baton and flipped him over, slamming him into the wall with my weight. I kicked his feet apart and slid the baton between his thighs, teasing it against his asshole until he moaned. I pressed him up against the wall and growled in his ear.

"Mine."

I stepped back and began to pound into his ass with the baton. There is something about that deep thud, right there, that feels like you are getting fucked. He groaned, leaning against the wall, offering his ass to me, luscious sounds leaving his lips with each strike of the baton. I stepped toward him and ground my cock into his ass, pulling him away from the wall.

"Stand up for me, boy. Take it."

I began to pound his biceps with the baton, watching the bruises blossom. He growled and stomped his feet as the blows continued, struggling to take it. As it went on, first one bicep, then the other, he shook his head and clenched his hands, eventually pounding his fists into his own sore thighs. I did not stop until his arms began to tremble.

When he's my boy, he doesn't want me to fuck around. He wants to be pushed to his physical limits, again and again. To constantly prove to himself (and to me) that he is tough enough, strong enough. That he can stand up and take anything I can dish out.

I set the baton down and pulled my belt from my jeans, snapping it.

"How many months have you been mine, boy?"

"Forty-two, Sir."

"That's right. Forty-two strokes it is. Count em for me."

"Yes, Sir."

My belt is serious business. It is always the last toy I pick up because it inspires my most intense sadism. The counting is as much for me as for him. This tool, more than any other, finds me wanting never to stop.

I grinned as the leather bit into his back, and went after his traps first. He was counting steadily as I hurled the belt at him, with a red haze around me and a metallic scent on his skin. I growled, driving the belt into his back, my cock throbbing, his voice grounding me. I stepped forward to rest my cheek against his back, heat rushing off his skin in waves, his adrenaline-soaked sweat setting off a sharp tang in the back of my throat. I snarled and rained fire onto his back with my belt in roaring relentless flames, no time between strokes, just one long maelstrom of energy building between us.

Some small part of my brain registered we were at thirty-seven. I stopped, wanting to savor the last five strokes. His breath was ragged, and he was shaking. I breathed in slowly, tasting the pain steaming off him, and sliced into him with all of my strength. Thirty-eight. Drove my hunger into him, raw and ravenous. Thirty-nine. Forty made him scream, sound pouring from him, rendering him unable to count.

"Take it for me, boy. Show me your strength. I know you can do it."

"Forty, Sir," he said shakily.

I growled the word "mine" as I ripped into him with my belt. Forty-one. I carved into his back, the full force of my weight behind the last blow. Forty-two. I wrapped the belt around the back of his neck, lifting it to his lips to kiss, as I pressed him into the wall, breathing him in.

"That's my boy. I am so proud you are mine," I whispered.

I unbuckled his belt and slid down his pants, letting him step out of them and lean against the wall in his jock.

"Stay right there, boy."

I pulled a chair over and sat in it, turning him to face me. I pulled out my cock, suited it up, and stroked on the lube. I placed his hands on the back of the chair and pulled his hips toward me, easing into his ass, his boots firmly planted on the floor. Damn, did he feel so fucking good.

"Stand up and ride my dick," I growled. He did, growling right back, jamming his ass onto me, riding my cock. He is a delicious fuck, and I told him so, a stream of obscenity pouring from my mouth and egging him on. He rammed his ass onto my cock so hard I began to close my eyes, my cheek resting on his shoulder, my nails gripping him, delighting in the feel of him riding me.

"That's it, boy. Fuck yourself on my cock. Show me how strong you are. Give me the ride of my life."

He was magic, my boy. Pulsing with intensity, his eyes locked onto mine, his jaw clenched as he worked his ass onto my cock, taking it into him, growling groans getting louder and louder.

"Mine," I snarled. "Mine. My boy. Hold your breath, clench down onto my cock, and come for me, boy."

I grabbed his hips and jammed him onto me as I came, feeling him shudder, pouring into him, feeling it build and build as he clamped down on my cock, clamped down on his breath. I held my own breath as long as I could until I released us both, holding his eyes and watching him explode when I ordered him to let it all go. He trembled from head to toe. His eyes held fireworks, feeding me, his hips riding me like there was no way to stop. It went on forever.

We slowly floated back into ourselves. I began to stroke his skin. It felt so amazing. I grinned into his eyes, hugging him close to me.

"You sure are strong, boy," I said, laughing delightedly. He grinned back at me. We breathed together, settling back into our own skin. I whispered praise in his ear as I stroked him, easing him off my cock gently and standing up to gather him close into a deep, wide-set hug that lasted a good long time.

UNWORTHY
AS I AM

Elizabeth Thorne

I waited for her on my knees, because I knew it would make her happy.

I waited naked and vulnerable, but also strong and certain, because I knew that I was precisely where I was meant to be.

I'd never been in love before—not like that. I might have thought I'd been, or lived a different color of emotion, but I'd never been able to warm my heart on just the thought of someone's name. It was the first time I'd fallen for someone so truly that even in my darkest hours, her existence was a beacon of light.

It terrified me.

I wanted to give her everything, and I had no idea how much she'd be willing to take.

Waiting wasn't a skill of mine. I could sit and work, still and silent with no regard for time, but to kneel and wait with nothing but her on which to muse was hard. I had to resist the urge to rise from my knees and pace. I had to fight the desire to jump to my feet every time I heard a car drive down the street. I felt like a dog waiting for her mistress, I was so anxious to see her again.

Use me—but as you would your spaniel, spurn me, strike me, neglect me, lose me; only give me leave to follow you... Suddenly Helena's motivation made a lot more sense. *The more you beat me, the more I will fawn on you* indeed. I wondered if there was any way for me to use that insight in my next book.

When I heard her footsteps on the stairs, it felt like I'd been waiting for years, and I took a deep breath and tried to find the quiet place she'd sculpted in my heart. I thought to myself, *this is for her,* and suddenly it blossomed. I let out my breath and with it the worries of the week. In my submission, I had finally found my patience.

My head bowed as she opened the door, and when I looked up I tried to let her see how I felt shining out of my eyes. It must have worked, because before even putting her satchel down, she took my chin in her hand and said, "Beautiful girl, I love you too."

After kissing me, quickly, and stroking her hand across my head, she put up her hand as though to tell me to stay. Then she put her bag down on the table by the front door and stepped out of my sight.

It felt odd to be so content simply because she was there. She made it home, although I'd lived there for almost a decade before we'd ever met—restless, discontent, successful, and alone. Then Karin had come into my life, and suddenly everything changed.

I will never forget the first night we met. We had both been attending one of *those* parties, her with some friends, me on my own. After an exceptionally stressful week of faculty meetings and final exams, I'd been hoping to pick someone up for a nice, lighthearted beating. Then I saw her.

She wasn't beautiful, but she was striking. Her short dark hair was cut in a masculine style, but she wore glittery earrings with her tailored suit, and she had a laugh like a glass of fine red wine—full-bodied and capable of knocking you under the table when you weren't paying attention. There was just something about her that drew me, although I had no idea who she was.

I went and found my best friend, Sam, the party's host, pointed out my mystery woman, and started pestering Sam for information. "What's her name? Is she a top?"

"Damned if I'd know," she said, "She's someone's plus one. I've never seen her before in my life."

When, fifteen minutes later, Karin took off a woman's dress and, with her enthusiastic consent, used a single tail on her until she bled, I watched, breathless, and nearly bit through my lip with longing and sorrow. Then, when the bottom's lover came up, kissed her happy partner deeply, and thanked my mystery woman for her help, I almost laughed in relief. All I could think was, *perhaps I have a chance with her after all.*

It made me uncomfortable to be so drawn to someone I didn't know, and instead of speaking with her when she looked up and caught my eye as she was putting away her toys, I fled to the kitchen to engage myself in the preparation of a proper cup of tea. When I glanced up from my detailed measurements, I realized she'd followed me.

"I saw you watching me," she said.

"It was a beautiful scene," I replied, staring intently at the print of a cat that was hanging on the wall behind her, unwilling to meet her eyes.

Suddenly I felt a touch on my chin and looked up to find sea green eyes staring down into mine. "You wanted it to be you."

I blushed and nodded.

"Next time, it could be," she said and then, handing me her

card, turned and walked out to rejoin the party.

I stared at her card in my hand. It was simple, but surprisingly elegant for something that was mostly black text on a white background. It had her name—Karin—a phone number, an e-mail address, and a stylized sketch of a woman holding a whip. *Karin*, I thought, *I can remember that,* and then I slipped the card into one of my knee-high boots and headed back out to the party.

Half an hour later, the ebb and flow of conversation had landed us in the same group. She'd walked up just as Sam was commenting on a piercing scene I'd bottomed to at her last party, and Karin immediately raised one eyebrow at me and said, "Oh! I love needles."

Remembering my earlier interest, Sam had unashamedly taken advantage of my blush and uncharacteristic silence to say, "You two should totally do a scene!" and then dragged the rest of the conversation off to another corner of the room.

"Good friend of yours?" Karin had asked me, smiling as she watched Sam and the other women walk away.

"Good...evil..." I smiled ruefully at my best friend's retreating form. "Sometimes it's hard to tell the difference. I'm Emily."

"Karin."

"I remember," I said, thinking of our moment in the kitchen, and then blushed again.

"It's all right," Karin said, taking a moment to look me up and down, from my glasses and bun to the tips of my brown granny boots, "I find you attractive too."

"I'm normally more erudite than this." I smiled quietly. "Ask anyone."

"I'd rather poke you with sharp pointy things," she said, gently running her fingers down my neck while watching my eyes to see if I'd object.

"Oddly enough," I blushed again, "I'd rather that too."

The next thing I knew, I was lying naked on a towel at the foot of Sam's bed, with one of the sexiest women I'd ever seen kneeling on top of my hips.

"Piercing for me," she'd said seductively as her hands gently swabbed my breasts with disinfectant, "is like fucking through skin."

My eyes had closed at the sound of her voice, and her statement made my thoughts go soft and liquid. I wasn't usually very submissive, but there was something about her that made me just want to give myself to her, to give her power. I let myself drift in her words as she finished preparing for the scene, and then I felt her hot breath by my ear.

"Do you want me inside you?" she whispered.

My breath caught. "Yes," I said. Perhaps I had been thinking less of needles in my breasts and more of fingers in my cunt, but I meant it all the same.

Then as I breathed out, she pushed the first needle in.

I gasped as I felt the first pop of the tip slipping under my skin, and she breathed with me as it slowly moved below the surface of my breast until she was where she wanted to finish the piercing.

"Are you ready?" she asked. "This is the part that hurts."

"I like it when the fucking hurts," I responded, and she laughed when I jerked as the now-duller tip once again pierced my skin, this time from the inside out.

"Oh, we are going to get along," she said, looking down at where the tip of the needle was just touching my nipple. Then she whispered in my ear, "I like to make it hurt a lot."

I held her eyes during the next needle, once she had started it in my skin, and it really had felt like she was fucking me with the piece of sharpened metal—the ache of the initial penetration, the feeling of it sliding inside me, the intimacy of her eyes on mine. By the time she had put in eight more, five in each breast, the towel beneath me was soaking wet, and we both were breathing fast.

"You like having me under your skin, don't you, girl?" Karin asked, carefully playing with my breasts so that I could feel the needles pulling inside me.

"Yes," I paused, "may I call you ma'am?" It hadn't been a question I had thought I would ask. Not, at least, of someone I just met.

Karin had stilled for a moment, stroking one of the needles where it lay beneath the surface of my breast. "Yes," she said, smiling thoughtfully, "I think you may."

"Yes, ma'am, I do."

That time it was Karin who had taken the deep breath. "Would you like having me in your mouth?" she'd asked, running one gloved finger across my lips.

In response, I opened my mouth and sucked her finger deep.

She stroked her finger down my cheek, asked, "Would you like having me in your cunt?" and all I could do was moan.

That was when I heard a gentle throat-clearing noise from by the door. Apparently Sam had been watching the scene, because she said, "Unfortunately, as much as I'd like to see that, it would be against the party rules."

"Oh, I know." Karin smiled wickedly down at me where I opened my eyes at the interruption of the moment. "I just wanted to know for future reference."

I glared up at her and then turned the look on Sam where she stood, laughing, in the door.

"Well, this one's a keeper," Sam said, and then she turned and walked out the door.

Karin brought my focus back to her by pushing deeply against the needles in my left breast.

"You were saying?" she asked.

"Yes."

Karin raised her eyebrow again.

"Ma'am."

"In the meantime," she grinned, "I'll just have to fuck your breasts."

That, after replacing the glove that had been in my mouth, was exactly what she did. She moved the needles so they pulled and tugged under my skin until the sensations had me writhing under her, and then she pulled them out one by one and dropped them into the sharps container. When the last one clattered into the plastic bin, we were both exhausted, and her hands were speckled with little dots of my blood.

"And now for the fun part," she said, and after grabbing my wrists in one hand to hold them to the bed, she picked up an alcohol swab in the other and began to run it across the surface of my breasts.

I'd been relatively quiet through the whole scene, but when the alcohol hit the first piercing, I screamed. The alcohol felt like fire every time it hit a spot of open skin, and I enjoyed fighting against her restraint almost as much as I loved the intense sensations of the pain.

By the time she finished cleaning us up, we were both out of breath, and after moving all of the sharp objects safely out of the way, Karin collapsed next to me on the bed.

"Was it good for you?" she asked, a goofy smile flashing across her face.

"Oh yes," I answered, and we lay there talking quietly until Karin's friend found her, let us know that it was after two a.m., and wondered aloud if it might be time to leave.

She smiled ruefully and touched my cheek gently before saying good-bye, and I fell asleep right where I lay. I barely woke up enough to move over when Sam crawled into her bed beside me and turned out the light.

The first thing I saw the next morning, when I woke up curled up next to my best friend, was Karin's card sitting on the floor, where it had fallen out of my boot. It had taken all the willpower I had to wait until I got home after work that evening to call her, and, amazingly, we've been together ever since.

My knees were beginning to ache from the cool tile floor when she finally returned to me, holding a cane of deep red Lucite.

I looked up at her with a question.

"You're in a quiet place tonight, aren't you, Emily?" she asked.

I nodded.

"But you're happy?"

I looked up at her, trying once more to let her see how I felt, and nodded again.

"Good." She smiled down at me. "Come lie down on the bed."

I rose to my feet as elegantly as I could and walked down the hallway to the bedroom. She'd pulled the covers back, and there was a pair of leather cuffs attached to the headboard and another pair at the footboard.

"I know you don't like to be bound," she said, "but if you wouldn't mind tonight... I don't have to lock them."

I shook my head and, catching the disappointed look in her eye, walked around to the nightstand. Rummaging around in it, I pulled out a small bag containing a quartet of brass locks and the matching key.

She glowed at me as I handed them to her, and asked me, "Truly?"

My answer was to climb up onto the bed and lie down on my

back, placing my wrists in the cuffs.

"Turn over, actually," she said, and then she locked my wrists and ankles into the restraints and started caning me.

I loved the cane, I always do. I loved the way she used it on me, building from a warm thuddy shower that felt more like sex than pain to deep, stinging blows that had me biting my lip and trying not to scream. Over and over, she'd build to the point where I was almost ready to give up, almost ready to ask her to stop, and then ease back down to an intensity that was easier to bear. She beat me for what felt like hours, until it felt like my ass and thighs were covered with bruises, until the pain and pleasure had become one and I thought that if she asked me to I could fly.

"I love doing this to you," she said, running her fingers over the welts she'd made, pinching and poking to make me squirm. "You're so beautiful when you're in pain. I love how much you give me." She dipped her fingers between my legs and found me drenched with desire. "I love how much you enjoy it."

"God, it turns me on to hurt you," she continued, moving her hand lower to stroke my clitoris and make me moan. "It makes me want to fuck you and hurt you even more."

"Please," I whispered into the pillow.

"What was that, girl?" I could smell my arousal on her fingers as she used them to turn my face to her ear.

"Please," I repeated.

"Since you ask so nicely," she said, "I suppose I will."

She walked around to the bottom of the bed, where I couldn't see her, and I heard the sounds of her buckling on her harness. Then I heard her rustling in the bedside drawer.

When she came back into view, she was nude except for the big green cock that curved up from the leather at her hips. It was her largest one, the one that hurt me if she used it for too long, and she smiled as she saw the fear and arousal in my eyes.

"Good girl," she said, "I'm going to roll you over now," and she released my ankles and did.

"Now," Karin continued, "I know this cock is going to hurt you when I fuck you, but it's not going to hurt enough, is it?" She pushed two fingers between my legs and they easily slid inside me. "You're already so wet that I know you'll need more." She continued to fuck me slowly with her fingers as she asked me, "Isn't that right?"

I blushed as I nodded my agreement, and she smiled.

"That's what I thought," she said, "which is why I took these out," and she held up a bag of fifty clothespins.

I shivered.

"Every one of them is going to go on you before I fuck you, and they're going to stay there until I'm done." She smiled down at me. "That's what you want, isn't it? For me to hurt you and fuck you until I'm through?"

It was, I realized, exactly what I wanted, but that didn't mean it didn't frighten me to agree.

Slowly she started to cover me with clothespins. First she placed painful lines across my breasts. Then, when she ran out of skin to torment, she started on my inner arms. After my arms my nipples, previously spared, were squeezed in a deep ache. Then the insides of my thighs, where she'd rub against them while she fucked me, were given five pins each. Two more pinched each earlobe and then, when I thought I could take no more, she clamped the final one right across my clitoris.

It was agonizing, and it was glorious. Constant, intense, and inescapable pain that rolled across me in waves, and I was ready to surrender to it until she started to fuck me.

Her cock hurt as it slid inside me, but it hurt in a different way than the clothespins. It hurt in a way that focused my attention on her. I looked up at Karin's face and saw her eyes gleam and her nipples harden every time I winced in pain, and it made me even more aroused. There was nothing more exciting to me than seeing her get turned on by hurting me. There was nothing better than knowing she was getting off on the pain her cock drew out of me as it pushed in deep against my cervix and then slid out to shove again home.

I began to beg, quietly, "Hurt me, please hurt me, use my pain to get yourself off, anything, I'll do anything," every time her hips slowed or her hands stopped moving across the clothespins covering my body, until she held her hands across my nose and mouth to quiet my screams as she worked my body until she was done with me—orgasming with her cock pressed deep inside me and tight against her clit.

I couldn't stop myself, and without a thought I came too, my body clenching tightly around her firm, green cock.

"I'm sorry!"

They were the loudest words that had come out of my mouth all night.

Karin looked concerned as she asked, "Why are you sorry?"

"I came without asking. I shouldn't have done that. I'm sorry." I felt like I was on the verge of tears, and looked away.

Karin turned my face toward hers. "I've never asked you for that. You don't have to apologize."

I tried to turn my face away, but she held me tight.

"Wait," she said, thoughtfully. "That's not why you're embarrassed." She paused. "It's because you want me to ask for that. You want to apologize."

"I'm sorry," I said again, my voice breaking, "It was wrong for me to presume."

"No, sweetheart," she said, "it wasn't wrong at all." She paused. "Do you want me to punish you?"

I nodded.

"Do you want to give me your orgasms?"

I blushed, and nodded again.

"Then this," she said, "is going to hurt."

"Every ten clothespins I take off," she continued, starting to pluck them from my body and causing little blooms of agony as sensation returned to each deprived nerve ending and aching piece of skin, "I'm going to fuck you to orgasm. I won't continue until you've come, and I'll keep going no matter how raw you are, or sore."

Her hips began to move as she took off the tenth clothespin, and I came almost immediately at the very thought of what she was suggesting.

She started on the next ten clothespins, and once again I came as soon as her hips began to move.

The third time it wasn't so easy. I was beginning to get tired; the pain from the release of the clothespins on my arms had overwhelmed my arousal, and the sensation of her cock inside me was making me feel bruised and sore. I didn't think I'd be able to come again until I saw the look of arousal at her eyes at the sight of the pain she was causing me, and it sent me over the edge.

The fourth time she had to fuck me for almost ten minutes, and the only thing that got me over the edge was desperation at the thought that I still had to do it again.

Then, when the only clothespin left was the one on my clitoris, she pulled her cock from my body and the sensation of emptiness was such a relief that I came again.

I could feel a look of horror fill my face, and she smiled at me.

"Yes, I saw that," she said, "and yes, you're going to have to pay."

Then she reached over to the nightstand drawer, smoothed a

condom over her cock, spread some lube onto it, and lifted my legs to press it against my ass.

I whimpered in fear.

"You've never taken this one up your ass before, have you, pretty girl?"

I shook my head.

"But you want to," she said. "You want me to fuck you like I said I would, as punishment until you come again."

I did. I was scared, I knew it would hurt, and I had never wanted anything more in my life.

I nodded, and she gently started to push into me.

It didn't hurt, not the way I feared. I was so turned on that although it felt big and scary, I was afraid I'd come from her using me before the clothespin was off, and that only aroused me more.

It took some time, but she slowly worked herself into my ass, and when her cock was buried as deeply as it would go, she pulled the clothespin off my clitoris and I screamed and came.

"Good girl," she said, and then her hips slowly started to move.

I gasped at the sensation of something so large fucking my ass and tried to relax into it as she smiled above me.

"This is for me," she said. "I'm just going to use that tight little hole of yours until I'm good and done with it, so you can come as much or as little as you like, I really don't care."

And I did. I came at the look of satisfaction and pleasure on her face as she fucked my ass. I came again when her hips pushed deeply, one last time inside me. Then I orgasmed once more when she pulled out and gathered me in her arms.

She snuggled me close until we both got our breath back. Then she asked me to kneel on the floor beside the bed and wait, before wandering from the room.

When she returned, she held something in her hands.

It was a collar.

Suddenly, for almost the first time since I'd known her, Karin looked nervous. "I hadn't planned to ask you yet. I didn't really think you were ready, but after tonight..." She paused. "Emily, would you do me the honor of wearing my collar?"

I looked at her, and suddenly my voice came out strong and clear. "In my heart," I said, "I think I already am."

ABOUT THE AUTHORS

ALYSIA ANGEL is a high femme currently living in Durham, North Carolina. She is a Lambda Literary 2011 Fellow, self-published, and published in *Salacious* magazine and *Curve* magazine. Alysia enjoys eating ribs with bare hands, food carts, reviewing restaurants, well-roasted coffee, and living the amoret dream.

RACHEL KRAMER BUSSEL (rachelkramerbussel.com) is an author, editor, blogger, and event organizer. She has edited over forty anthologies, including *Women in Lust, Best Bondage Erotica 2011* and *2012, Spanked, Bottoms Up, Orgasmic, Fast Girls, The Mile High Club,* and more. She's a sex columnist for *SexIs* magazine and blogs at lustylady.blogspot.com and cupcakestakethecake.blogspot.com.

SOSSITY CHIRICUZIO is a working-class/fat/poly femme who hosts and produces Dirty Queer, a monthly X-rated open mic, fund-raiser, and community gathering. She has a CD,

Hand to Mouth, and released *Stir The Juice*, a book of erotic poetry about queer passion and adventure, in 2011.

KIKI DELOVELY is a queer femme performer/writer whose work has appeared in *Best Lesbian Erotica 2011* and *2012*, *Salacious* magazine, *Gotta Have It: 69 Stories of Sudden Sex*, and *Take Me There: Transgender and Genderqueer Erotica*. Kiki's greatest passions include artichokes, words, alternative baking, and taking on research for her writing.

SHAWNA ELIZABETH (fuckyeahfemmes.tumblr.com) is a femme writer and academic studying queer theory. This is her first time writing smut.

GIGI FROST (www.thefemmeshow.com) is a Boston-based artist and activist who serves up smut with a side of politics. She tours nationally with Body Heat and The Femme Show. Recent publications under a variety of pseudonyms include *Second Person Queer* and *Girl Crazy*.

MERIDITH GUY (meridithguy.tumblr.com) lives with her partner in rural Virginia where they do very naughty things behind closed doors in their very nice neighborhood. She has many hobbies with a kinky bent, building sawhorses among them.

DUSTY HORN's erotica has been published by Cleis in *Orgasmic* and *Best Bondage 2011*, her sex culture reportage on CarnalNation.com, and her critical theory of sex work in *AORTA* magazine. A BDSM professional, queer pornographer, kink educator, social worker, and rocknroll exhibitionist slut, Dusty is (in)famous for her spanking booths.

AUGUST INFLUX (augustinflux.wordpress.com) is brand new to the wonderful world of writing. By day, she wanders around San Jose State University (California) campus as Big Queer Activist. By night she hides in her Bat Cave and homeworks it up until the wee hours of the morning. On weekends, she dons the guise of a housewife and bakes up a storm in her apron and high heels. She loves being femme, as a boy or a girl, and thinks monogamy as it relates to her is silly.

WENDI KALI is a part-time writer and photographer and full-time motorcycle-riding butch. She is currently working on a manuscript about her life as a gender-bending butch. "First Ride" is her first publication. She currently lives in Portland, Oregon.

DILO KEITH is a polymorphously perverse bisexual queer, thanks, in part, to Brenda Howard. Writing erotica is the newest manifestation of a lifelong fascination with sexuality and multi-decadal interest in BDSM. It felt great the first time, so Dilo did it again, first alone, later with friends, and eventually in public.

Editor of *Carnal Machines, Spank, The Sweetest Kiss,* and *Where the Girls Are*, **D. L. KING** has contributed short stories to *Best Lesbian Erotica, Best Women's Erotica, Girl Crazy,* and *Broadly Bound*, among others. She's published two novels and edits the erotica review site *Erotica Revealed*. Find her at www.dlkingerotica.com.

VIE LA GUERRE is a femme wordsmith who lives in Chicago with her kitten, Foxy Brown.

SASSAFRAS LOWREY (www.PoMoFreakshow.com) is an international award–winning storyteller, author, artist, and educator. Sassafras is the editor of the *Kicked Out* anthology, which brought together the voices of current and former homeless LGBTQ youth. Her prose has been included in numerous anthologies and she regularly teaches LGBTQ storytelling workshops at colleges and conferences across the country. Sassafras lives in Brooklyn, New York, with her family.

ELAINE MILLER (www.ElaineMiller.com) is a Vancouver leatherdyke who has been passionately involved in the leather/queer community for eighteen years through writing, education, and creating events. As a writer, Elaine has been frequently anthologized and spent four years as a kinky sex columnist. She runs a wee brick-and-mortar store selling consignment leathers to bikers and leatherfolk.

MIRIAM ZOILA PÉREZ is a Cuban-American writer, blogger, and reproductive justice activist. She is the founder of Radical Doula.com and an editor at Feministing.com. Her essays have been included in various anthologies, including *Persistence: All Ways Butch and Femme*. Pérez lives in Brooklyn.

BB RYDELL promotes queer visibility, expression, and grassroots community building through writing, filmmaking, and performance. Rydell co-produces Seattle Spit, Seattle's longest-running monthly queer spoken-word event, and is a member of the Producers Collective, an intentional artist and producer community that values social justice, creative expression, and diversity. Rydell's work has been screened at the Seattle Transgender Film Festival and is published in *Tales of Travelrotica: Volume 2* and *Penetalia*.

MARIA SEE is a Brooklyn native living in San Francisco. Her writing has been published in collections including *Visible: A Femmethology* and *Gotta Have It: 69 Stories of Sudden Sex.* She is currently working on her first book, a novel of erotic dominance and submission.

ELIZABETH THORNE is thrilled to make her living from sex...writing about it, that is. In addition to working as a sex educator, she has contributed to numerous erotic anthologies. Her collection of pansexual BDSM erotic fairy tales—*The Gingerbread Dungeon*—was published in July 2011. Learn more at WithBatedBeth.com.

AMELIA THORNTON is a very good girl with very bad thoughts, who lives by the English seaside with her collection of school canes, a lot of vintage lingerie, and too many shoes. She has been published in *Best Women's Erotica 2011* and *2012*, *Women in Lust,* and several Xcite anthologies, and enjoys baking, hard spankings, and writing beautiful naughtiness.

ANNA WATSON is a married old-school femme mom who queers suburbia west of Boston. For more, see *Sometimes She Lets Me; Girl Crazy; Best Lesbian Erotica 07, 08, 09; Fantasy: Untrue Stories of Lesbian Passion; Visible: A Femmethology, Volume One;* and *Take Me There.* As Cate Shea, she writes for www.customeroticasource.com.

XAN WEST is the pseudonym of an NYC BDSM/sex educator. Xan's "First Time Since" won honorable mention for the 2008 NLA John Preston Short Fiction Award. Xan has appeared in many anthologies, including *Best SM Erotica 2 & 3, Best Women's Erotica 2008 & 2009,* and *Best Lesbian Erotica 2011.*

ABOUT
THE EDITOR

SINCLAIR SEXSMITH (mrsexsmith.com) is a writer, performer, and teacher focused on sovereignty, healing, and communication through the personal examinations of sex, gender, and relationships. She has written the award-winning personal online writing project *Sugarbutch Chronicles: The Sex, Gender, and Relationship Adventures of a Kinky Queer Butch Top* at Sugarbutch.net since 2005. Her smut stories can be found in more than a dozen anthologies, including *Best Lesbian Erotica 2006, 2007, 2009,* and *2011; Secret Slaves: Erotic Stories of Bondage; Gotta Have It: 69 Stories of Sudden Sex; Sometimes She Lets Me: Best Butch/Femme Erotica; The Harder She Comes: Butch Femme Erotica;* and *Take Me There: Transgender and Gender-queer Erotica.* Her writings on gender are included in *Visible: A Femmethology Volume II* and *Persistence: All Ways Butch and Femme.* She writes online in various places, including butch perspective on pop culture at AfterEllen.com, advice at SexIs-Magazine.com, and Cliterotica, a lesbian erotica roundup, for the Lambda Literary Foundation. Mr. Sexsmith holds degrees in both social change and creative writing from the University of Washington, and studied and taught writing and performance poetry at the Bent Writing Institute for queers in Seattle. From her current home of New York City she produces Sideshow: The Queer Literary Carnival reading series. This is her first anthology.